KARMA IS A BITCH

LUST, LIES AND THE DEADLY CONSEQUENCES OF BETRAYAL

SHOME MAK

To those who inspired it

and will not read it

Contents

Contents

About The Author

Shome Mak is a filmmaker with over 15 years of experience in the entertainment industry, known for creating the Bollywood film '**Blind**'. Born and raised in Mumbai, he developed a love for storytelling at an early age, which has driven his passion for both film and writing. With a keen eye for the complexities of human relationships, Shome explores themes of love, betrayal, and karma in his work. When not behind the camera, he immerses himself in the written word, crafting tales that captivate and provoke thought. *Karma is a Bitch* marks his debut novel, where he blends his cinematic vision with the art of fiction.

PROLOGUE

It's been eight long years since that pivotal day. The world has undergone drastic changes: democracies eroded into dictatorships, roads laid over the oceans, robots edging close to dominance, and humanity teetering on the brink of extinction. Yet, my thirst for revenge remains as fierce as ever. I once hoped it would wane over time, fade into the background, but I was mistaken. Closure eludes me still, and I doubt I'll find peace until I confront the past head-on.

It's unjust, you see... No one should endure such suffering... It simply isn't right... Individuals like that have no place in our world. They say karma comes full circle, but how long must one wait for justice? Forever? As Wayne Dyer aptly stated, "How people treat you is their karma; how you react is yours." She acted as she saw fit, and now it's my turn to respond. I must forge my own destiny, write my own conclusion. No one will do it for me. I'll be judge, jury, and executioner. Unlike Maximus, I will have my vengeance in this life, not the next.

I

MIKE

As I lay back in the cozy leather recliner of the Mumbai International airport lounge, sipping on a neat Talisker 18-year-old, my eyes caught a glimpse of the television screen in front of me. The volume had been turned down but the picture of me was splashed across the screen for everyone to see. I noticed a few curious passengers throw looks in my direction to try and figure out if it is indeed me that they see on the screen. The banner under the picture read, 'Mikesh Kharbanda, writer of the bestselling novel – Life: Beyond Reality, is being honoured with the prestigious Baillie Gifford prize.'

I spent a year of my life reading all the self-help books I could lay my hands on to try and find inspiration to write one of my own. I always expected that my first novel would be a thriller, but after 3 years of failing to impress publications with my ideas, I made a decision to follow the 'trend'. Covid really fucked people up and the publications cashed in on it by spitting out one self-help book after another. Mental health was all anyone could talk about during those traumatic years while self-help book writers raked in the spoils of that trauma. Not wanting to miss the money train, I jumped right on it. Honestly, I didn't know the first thing about writing a self-help book, but luckily enough, other writers did. It was relatively simple to pick up bits and pieces from other books and piece them together to create something worthy of a Baillie Gifford Prize. Fortunately, I was smart enough to not get called out because if you really look into it, most self-help books say the same things in a slightly different way.

Of the handful of people shooting looks in my direction, one pair of eyes caught my attention. They were sun-kissed brown eyes with lashes longer than I'd seen before. From where I was sitting, it was tough to tell if they were real or stuck on. The rest of her face was just as beautiful as her eyes. If there was an app to create the perfect girl, she would be the cover model. Even from the neck down, though she was sitting, I could tell that she's someone I'd like to join the mile-high club with. The white shirt underneath the blazer of her slate grey skirt suit had enough buttons open to keep you from looking away. She was the kind of attractive that would even reject a guy in his own dream. I've been told that I'm quite the looker myself, but even I would think twice before walking up to a woman like that. I struggled to take my eyes off her cleavage. Thankfully, apart from the one moment when our eyes met, she'd been too engrossed in her book to notice.

If I could fast-forward time and take a look into the future, I'd have never looked in her direction. It's strange how a fleeting attraction can spiral into something far more dangerous, how one glance can lead you down a path you never intended to take. If someone had told me that a single encounter on a flight could unravel my life, I'd have laughed it off. To be fair, my agent did warn me about it, but boys will be boys, right? I wish I just kept my head down, focused on my drink, and never looked up.

My moment in 'Life: Beyond Reality' was cut short by the airport attendant telling me that it's time to board the flight. I downed the remainder of my Talisker and hopped off the recliner in the coolest way that I could. She was still too engrossed in her book to notice. I watched the attendant walk over to the girl of my dreams to pass on the same information. I left the lounge with the hope that God, if there was one, would be kind enough to put her in seat 1B. A prayer that I would eventually come to regret. It would be a lot easier to initiate a conversation with her if she was seated next to me. Praise the Lord!

II

NATASHA

I knew that the man sitting a few recliners away is the same one whose face was splashed across the news channel. He kept glancing at the screen, then at the other people in the lounge, all the while pretending he's unfazed by the news coverage of his Baillie Gifford Prize win. He wasn't not doing a great job of hiding his excitement. I was definitely playing it cooler. He had been staring at me for almost five minutes straight without blinking. I considered buttoning up my shirt, but I also enjoy the attention. He was a strikingly handsome man. I've always had a soft spot for guys with long hair. Even through his sports jacket, it was clear he works out. And I couldn't fault him for staring at my cleavage. It's a good cleavage; everyone stares, so why not him? My body, my rules, right?

I had read Mikesh Kharbanda's book, Life: Beyond Reality, when it first came out. I was hooked from the first chapter and devoured it in a single sitting. The honestly, the depth – everything about it felt like it was speaking directly to me. I remember trying to find him on social media afterward, hoping to get a glimpse into the mind of the man who had written something so profound. There's wasn't much to find, just a few interviews and sparse posts, but it was enough for me to develop an instant crush. He was mysterious, intellectual, and now, apparently, award-winning. When I read about his Baillie Gifford prize win a year later, I was thrilled and hoped that I might get a chance to meet him in London. But as fate would have it, the universe worked faster than I expected, putting us on the same flight.

I heard the airport attendant tell him it's time to board, but I lingered a minute longer, pretending to be absorbed in my book. I didn't want my interest in him to be too obvious, at least not yet. I know I'm attractive and I know how to use it to my advantage. And I do, when the time is right. The way he slid off his recliner, trying to look cool – it was clearly a show just for me, but I acted like my book had all my attention. I waited patiently for the attendant to come over and give me the same boarding cue. I was hoping he was in seat 2A. I thought it would be a great opportunity to give him something to write about. Who knew that thought would become a reality.

I walked down the aisle of the business class section, my Chanel tote hanging off one shoulder and my book tucked under my arm. I spotted Mikesh as he settled into seat 1A. So close. Striking up a conversation with someone seated in the row ahead wouldn't be easy. I walked up to my seat and placed my bag on it. The seat next to mine was empty; being the last person to board the flight, I knew it would stay that way for the entire nine-hour journey to London. I leaned over slightly to catch a glimpse of the person in 1B, next to Mikesh. A slightly chubby, short fellow – sort of like a young Danny DeVito. I knew it was going to be an easy switch.

I made sure my shirt was open just enough to sway his decision, then gently placed my hand on his shoulder. "Hi... Would you be willing to switch seats? It's the one right behind. In fact, the seat next to it is empty too, so you can have your pick." I leaned forward slightly, giving him a better view, and flashed my warmest smile. Mr. DeVito took a moment to process that I'm actually standing in front of him, then, without a word, he unbuckled his seatbelt and offered me his seat. Mikesh watched this interaction with a suppressed smile. I was almost certain that if I hadn't made the switch, he would have. I took my seat and fastened my seatbelt. Mikesh smiled politely at me, and I returned the smile.

"Mother! Whose virgin bosom was uncrost, with the least shade of thought to sin allied. Woman! Above all women glorified, our tainted nature's solitary boast." Of all the opening lines Mikesh could have used, this was the last I expected. He gave me a full smile, looking like a cross between Hrithik Roshan and Bradley Cooper. It was tough not to stare.

"The Virgin! William Wordsworth." Luckily, I know my poetry. Mikesh was impressed. Score: Mikesh 1, Natasha 1. "Speaking of Virgins...."

I noticed Mikesh looking past me. I turned to see Mr. DeVito standing by my seat, staring at my face – or more accurately, about six inches south of it. DeVito shifted his gaze to Mikesh.

"This isn't a bus. You're going to need to sit down."

It took a moment for Mr. DeVito to register the comment. Embarrassed and awkward, he turned back to me and handed me my Chanel Tote.

"You left this on my seat... I mean your seat, which I am now sitting on... I'm meant to sit on."

He was mumbling and fumbling, the words struggling to find their way out of his mouth. I took the bag from his hand.

"Thank you so much."

I flashed another smile at him. His smile was crooked and childish. He glared at Mikesh and then walked back to his seat. I turned to Mikesh. It was my move now.

"Seems like he was living life beyond reality for a second there."

One of Mikesh's eyebrows rose higher than the other, just like The Rock.

"I see you've read my books."

I pulled out the book tucked between my leg and the armrest and held it up in front of him. 'Life: Beyond Reality by Mikesh Kharbanda.'

"Guilty as charged. The prestigious Baillie Gifford Prize-winning author, Mr. Mikesh Kharbanda." I said with a flirty smile.

"Well, technically, not till 8 p.m. tomorrow". He extended his hand. "Mike, my friends call me Mike."

I reached out and shook his hand, noting his firm grip. "Natasha, my friends call me Black Widow."

He looked me up and down, then once more before he spoke.

"Well, minus the latex, I think that's pretty accurate."

The captain asked the crew to take their stations for take-off, and moments later, we're high up in the sky, on our way to London. Mike and I made some small talk until the flight attendant brought us our glasses of champagne. He placed the glasses in front of us. I raised my glass for a toast, and Mike followed suit.

"Here's to a happy life, an easy death, honest relationships and minty fresh breath."

Mike let out a big laugh at my playful toast. "You should be a writer," he said.

I maintained eye contact as I took a sip of my champagne. I knew he was the kind to take a hint. But, just to be sure, I wanted my intentions to be crystal clear.

"I shall ponder on that thought as I use the little girl's room."

I placed my glass of champagne on the tray in front of me and undid my seat belt. Bending over to slip my shoes back on, which I had sneakily kicked off earlier, I offered him a tantalizing glimpse of the world he was about to experience. Just as I was about to get up, I turned to Mike...

"But..."

He seemed intrigued.

"But?" he asked, with utmost curiosity.

"But..." I lingered a little. "I have a little paranoia when it comes to using the facilities of an airplane."

Now, I had his full attention. Not to say that I didn't before, but now, it was all eyes on me.

"And what paranoia might that be?" There was a glint in his eye as he waited for my response. I flashed a flirty smile in his direction.

"I'm always afraid that someone might walk in when I'm there."

Mike leaned in a little closer to me.

"I'm going to let you in on a little secret. On the inside of the door, there's a little nob that you can turn. It secures entry into that space, and you can use the facilities without fear."

Now it was my turn. I leaned in even closer. We were only a few inches apart.

"That's the thing though... I always forget." And that was my cue to make my exit.

I got up and walked away as slowly as I could, giving him plenty of time to appreciate the results of all the hard work I put in at the gym, as I made my way to the bathroom.

III

MIKE

I've been an atheist for as long as I can recall. Despite my parents' religious beliefs, they never imposed them on me. I vividly remember the day I disclosed my atheism to them, just a week after my 17th birthday, and eight months before their planned trip to New York and Geneva. Surprisingly, they weren't troubled by my choice; rather, they supported it wholeheartedly. They believed it was crucial for me to forge my own path, whether God found a way into my life or not. That day, I wished I could share with my mother that I had discovered my own connection with God, technically, a Goddess. It saddened me that she wasn't there to witness my transformation into a believer. Unfortunately, their journey from New York to Geneva on September 2nd, 1999, never reached its destination. I was under the care of my Uncle Arun at the time. I can still recall that day as if it were yesterday. Returning from my guitar lesson, I sat in the living room practicing while Uncle Arun watched the news. Swissair Flight 111 tragically plummeted into the sea off Nova Scotia, Canada, during its night journey, claiming the lives of all 229 passengers on board. What was intended as a two-week stay with Uncle Arun extended to two years until I departed for the University of Manchester to pursue my MA in creative writing.

My interest in writing blossomed shortly after my parents' tragic accident. It became my outlet for the immense pain I was experiencing. When I expressed my desire to become a writer and apply at the University of Manchester to Uncle Arun, he readily agreed. The insurance payout from my parents' life insurance policy enabled him to afford sending me there, and for us to live a better life than we were living at the time. If it wasn't for that payout, I wouldn't be able to afford to spend 18 years trying to be a writer. Although I briefly experimented with writing for ad agencies, the allure of penning a book captivated me more. If COVID hadn't blindsided us the way it did, I might have still been grappling with the challenges of getting published. However, thanks to Life: Beyond Reality, every publication in the country was clamouring for my next book. My dream of writing a thriller was finally materializing, but not without its own set of problems though.

Observing her stride towards the toilet, I couldn't help but notice her toned physique – either the result of countless hours at the gym or a blessing from the heavens themselves. Initially, I thought entering the mile-high club would require considerable effort, but it seemed she was just as eager, if not more so. As I approached the toilet door, I quickly scanned the business class section, finding most passengers asleep, except for one pair of eyes fixed on me: my former seatmate, Mr. DeVito, his expression far from pleased with our antics. Suddenly, a hand shot out from the toilet, gripping my jacket and yanking me inside.

Natasha's jacket was off and one more button on her white shirt has been undone. We were mere inches apart, her breath grazing my neck. This facility was not built to accommodate more than one person.

"I've always toyed with the idea of joining the mile-high club… but it seemed like a logistical nightmare. However, my perspective is shifting", I admitted with a grin, leaning in for a kiss. Just as our lips were about to meet, her finger appeared, pressing against my lips and pushing me back – about five and a half inches, to be precise.

"The interesting thing about cramped spaces is… You really gotta know how to use them."

She hiked her skirt up a bit and perched on the sink. One of her leg's rested on the edge of the throne, while the other pressed against the door. It was a moment ripe for seizing. I gently placed my hands on her thighs, tracing them upward beneath her skirt until I encountered lace. The thought of removing her thong crosses my mind, but closing an open door felt wrong. I opted to manoeuvre around it instead. Leaning in close to her ear, I whispered softly.

"If at any point you feel faint, dizzy or out of breath, let me know and I'll go faster."

She bit down on her lower lip in anticipation as I slowly kneeled down in front of her. My eyes were locked with hers as I inched closer. Her fingers were tangling in my hair, urging me closer. I planted soft kisses along her inner thighs, savouring the way her breath hitched with each touch. My lips moved slow, with purpose, teasing her with the promise of what's to come. She moaned, her hips arching towards me. I took my time, drawing out the moment, letting the anticipation build until it was almost unbearable. Finally, my tongue found its way past her thong, and she moaned louder, a sound that sent a surge of electricity through me. I started with gentle strokes, testing her reactions, feeling her body respond to my touch. I pressed my tongue against her, finding the rhythm that made her gasp and moan. Her legs began to tremble, her breaths coming faster, and I knew she was close. I maintained my pace, my hands gripping her thighs to steady her. Her climax hit like a tidal wave, her cries echoing off the bathroom walls. Her fingers clenched in my hair, her entire body quaking. When she finally still, I pulled back, looking up to see the satisfied, dazed expression on her face. She pulled me up into a deep kiss. The world outside the bathroom faded away, leaving just us, caught in the heat of our stolen moment. She leaned in close to me.

"I just got a glimpse of life beyond reality." Her words came out soft and shaky.

She hopped off the sink, and in one swift, graceful motion, almost like a dance move, she flipped our positions around. Now, I was leaning against the sink. Her hands went straight to my waistband, gripping the button of my trousers. With a practiced ease, she undid the button. The sound of the zipper coming down was almost deafening in the confined space. My heart raced, pounding so hard I swear I could see it through my shirt. She looked deep into my eyes, and I was lost in the intensity of her gaze.

"Sit back and enjoy the..."

KNOCK! KNOCK! Our moment was interrupted by an ill-timed knock on the door.

"There's someone in here," I yelled out hoping to send the person away, but a voice came yelling right back.

"I know what you two are doing in there... Some people actually need to use the facilities you know."

I was so tempted to throw some curses in his direction, but before I could even think of what to say, I heard the sound of the zipper going the other way. It's funny how I never noticed that a zipper sounds different when it's being pulled up versus when it's being pulled down. I turned to Natasha, who had a sheepish smile on her face.

"I guess we'll never know how this story ends."

Unlocking the bathroom door, she swung it open, revealing our pudgy acquaintance from seat 2B. Exiting awkwardly, we made room for Mr. DeVito as he squeezed uncomfortably past us to enter. The sign on the door switched from 'Vacant' to 'Occupied.' While I may not have officially joined the mile-high club, I had certainly aced the entrance exam.

IV
NATASHA

I love the air in the London, there's something about it that makes me feel alive. I can't explain it, but it's there. Some of the thrill I was feeling was probably from my little escapade on the flight, but the rest of it was all London. This city has always held a special place in my heart. I did my first ever solo trip here back in 2004. I was just eighteen, fresh out of college, and ready to explore the world. I stayed in a cozy little hostel near Covent Garden, and every morning, I'd wake up early, eager to soak in every bit of the city's charm. I wandered through the cobblestone streets, marvelled at the grandeur of Buckingham Palace, and spent hours getting lost in the endless corridors of the British Museum.

One of my fondest memories is sitting on the steps of the National Gallery, eating a simple lunch of fish and chips wrapped in paper, while watching the street performers entertain the crowds. I still remember the woman performing "Everything" by Alanis Morissette.

As the sun set, I would walk along the Thames, the city lights shimmering on the water, and I felt a sense of belonging I'd never experienced before. London was more than just a city to me; it was a revelation, a place where I discovered my independence and fell in love with the idea of adventure. Every time I return, the same excitement washes over me. The city has changed, and so have I, but the magic remains. London, with its blend of history and modernity, continues to be my favourite escape, a reminder of the fearless young girl who took her first solo trip and found a sense of belonging that never existed before.

I was raised by my father, a man constantly on the move, wrapped up in the demands of his business. My mother died during childbirth, so I never knew her touch or her voice. Instead, my world was shaped by our nanny, who became my constant caregiver and surrogate mother.

My father, despite his frequent absences, ensured I had everything I could ever ask for. Expensive toys, the best schools, lavish vacations – materially, I wanted for nothing. But no amount of money ever bought a minute of time. He was a figure seen more often in photographs and fleeting visits than in daily life. I craved for his attention. I consider that to be a big reason for my career choice. I just wanted to be noticed.

A year ago, during the chaos of COVID, my father passed away. It was a quiet death, unremarkable in the grand scheme of the pandemic's toll, but it marked the end of an era for me. Despite his emotional distance, his presence has been a constant, like the background hum of a machine, Now, even that was gone.

As I stepped out of the airport with Mike escorting me to my car, I couldn't stop replaying our encounter in my head. I was tempted to ask for another meeting, but I was hoping he would take the initiative. We hadn't spoken much since our little escapade in the bathroom; he slept through the rest of the flight. I might have worn him out. With Mr.

DeVito's eyes on us, there was no going back in for round 2.

My Burton stroller trailed behind me as we arrived at my car. Mike stepped forward and opened the door for me. Chivalry isn't dead. Just as I was about to get in, Mike broke the silence, saying exactly what I hoped he would.

"Can I see you again?" I could see the eagerness on his face.

"To finish where we left off?" I asked with a playful smile.

"Well... First, a date." I was impressed.

"A date? Wow, really?"

He flashed his Bradley Cooper smile at me. "Yeah, I want to do this right. A nice dinner at a fancy restaurant. A bottle of the Domaine Leroy Chambertin from the Cote de Nuits vineyard in France... followed by some over-the-trousers action in the car ride back to mine."

That last bit caught me by surprise, but I liked it. He had a sense of humour, and that's always important. I definitely wanted to see him again, but I wanted to make him sweat a little before I said yes. Without a word, I got into the car and shut the door. I saw the look of disappointment on his face through the window. My driver put the car in drive and started to inch forward. I asked him to go slowly. Mike dropped his head and began to walk away. I had played this out long enough. I pushed the button on the side of the door to bring down the window, but only halfway.

"Hey," I called out to Mike. He turned around and looked at me, hope in his eyes. "Duck and Waffle at Bishopsgate. 8 p.m." His eyes lit up. Before he could respond I pushed the button the other way and closed the window.

Five minutes into the car ride to my Airbnb, it hit me like a ton of bricks. "Technically, not till 8 p.m. tomorrow." That's what he said to me on the flight last night. I realized that

I had invited him to dinner at the exact same time as the Baillie Gifford Prize event. Seriously, fuck my life. I thought it would be more mysterious not to exchange numbers, and now I had no way of contacting him to reschedule. He was certainly not going to skip his award function for a girl he just met on the plane, no matter how hot she is.

Great. I had essentially set myself up for a romantic dinner for one, with a side of public humiliation. I thought maybe I could take a selfie with his empty chair and caption it, "Waiting for Mr. Baillie Gifford Prize winner."

But then, a thought struck me: the world runs on hope, and so do I. Despite the risk of him not showing up, I decided to go anyway. If nothing else, I would have a fabulous dinner with a spectacular view. And who knows? Maybe the universe would take pity on me for once. Worst case, I would have a great story to tell – like that time I got stood up by a Baillie Gifford Prize winner. Stranger things have happened, right?

V

MIKE

I just stood there, watching the car drive away, faced with one of life's greatest dilemmas. Do I go to Guildhall and collect my Baillie Gifford Prize for the best-selling novel – Life: Beyond Reality; or do I go to Duck and Waffle and actually live life beyond reality? The moment of truth. I pondered that thought during the car ride to my hotel. How is one expected to make such a difficult life decision in less than half a day.

On the one hand, I could go to the ceremony, make my publisher and agent very happy, but break a poor girl's heart. On the other hand, I could disappoint my agent and publisher, who are disappointed enough as it is by the absences of any pages from my second book, and experience something I may never get a chance to again. I could always win another award, but a girl like Natasha, she was a once-in-a-lifetime thing. And thank God for that. No one should have the opportunity to meet a girl like that more than once-in-a-lifetime.

Duck and Waffle at Bishopsgate – what a place. Perched high above London on the 40th floor, it was a blend of urban sophistication and cozy charm. The restaurant offered a stunning view of the sparkling skyline of the city. The menu was quirky yet refined, with dishes like their signature duck and waffle, a perfect mix of sweet and savoury. The vibe was vibrant, yet there was an intimacy that makes you feel like you're in on a well-kept secret. It was the kind of place where moments turn into memories, and that night, was the stage for what could be the most unforgettable night of my life. Looking back, I'd give anything to be able to erase that entire chapter from my life's story.

As I walked in, my eyes were immediately drawn to a circular booth by the window, and there she was – Natasha, looking like a goddess. She was wearing a black, low-cut dress that hugged her curves perfectly, the city lights casting a soft glow on her. The dress was elegant, yet daring, sophisticated but with an edge that matched her personality. It was clear she dressed to impress, and she was succeeding spectacularly. The night got a whole lot more interesting.

Natasha waved at me from the booth, as I made my way towards her. My phone started to vibrate inside the pocket of my white sports jacket as I approached the table. I pulled it out – 'Agent calling.' I gave her a quick hug followed by an apologetic look.

"Sorry, I need to take this. It might be a minute."

She smiled at me. "Of course, you've given up a lot to be here, please, take it." I smiled as we both took our seats and I answered my phone. I tried to sound convincingly miserable as I spoke with my Agent.

"Yeah, I'm really sorry about missing the ceremony. I must've caught something on the flight. Felt terrible all day." I faked a cough, hoping to sound pathetic enough to elicit sympathy from him. His voice crackled through the phone, thick with disappointment, telling me how disastrous it was. Natasha, across from me, gave me a sly smile and raised an eyebrow. That black, low-cut dress, looking even more provocative under the restaurant's ambient lighting. She took a sip of her water, then deliberately dropped her fork.

"I know, I know. But what could I do? I was in no shape to – "

Natasha slid under the table. My heart started to race as I realized her intention. I could hear my agent calling out to me on the other end of the line. For a second there I almost forgot he was on the call. "Yeah, I'm still here. Just... really worn out."

Natahsa's fingers trailed up my legs. I grip my phone tighter, struggling to maintain my composure. I could hear my agent saying something about doing damage control, but my attention was split between him and Natasha's antics under the table. She had about eighty percent of my attention. "Y-yeah, sure," I stammered, as Natasha's hands continued their journey, reaching my knees. Her eyes locked onto mine with a mischievous glint. My agent's voice faded into the background as Natasha unzipped my trousers and freed me from my boxers. I sucked in a breath, struggling to keep my voice steady. "I – I understand. I'll do whatever it takes." Natasha's lips wrapped around me, and it took every ounce of willpower not to let out a moan. I bit my lip, gripping the edge of the table. My agent mumbled more things that I couldn't quite comprehend. Maybe he was clear, and my brain refused to process the words that came through. I barely managed to hang up before a low groan escaped my lips. Natasha's movements were slow, deliberate, sending waves of pleasure coursing through me. She looked up, her eyes full of playful defiance. I couldn't help but smile down at her, grateful that I chose to skip the ceremony. Who needs a Baillie Gifford Prize when you have a goddess like Natasha, turning every moment into an unforgettable experience?

Natasha's head popped up on the other side of the table. She took a quick look around to see if anyone caught her in the act. She held up the fork that was in her hand and placed it back on the table. "Took a while, but I managed to find it." Her eyes were fixed on me. I took a sip of my water. "Maybe it's my turn to drop a fork." Natasha held her gaze, not saying a word. I was not sure what was going on in that brain of hers, so I decided to ask. "What is it? Why are you looking at me like that?"

"Are you going to tell your wife about this?"

What the fuck? Did she just ask me about my wife?

VI

NATASHA

Mike's jaw dropped to the floor; his surprise evident as he searched for a response. It was almost amusing watching him struggle. Ah, but here came the waiter, a welcome interruption. A moment to gather his thoughts. And then, his attention shifted to the extravagant bottle of wine, a diversion from the awkwardness of the moment.

"As promised, A bottle of the Domaine Leroy Chambertin from the Cote de Nuits vineyard of France. I pre-ordered it for our date," he said. Mike seemed rather pleased with himself. The server poured a little wine into a glass. About 13 ml. He handed it to Mike. Mike pointed towards me. The waiter placed the glass next to me and waited for me to sample the burgundy liquid floating around in it. I took a sip of the Domaine Leroy Chambertin, letting it dance on my tongue before swallowing. It was like tasting a symphony. Rich blackberries and cherries hit me first, followed by this beautiful earthiness, like walking through a damp forest. I could detect a hint of truffle, a touch of spice, and the tannins were incredibly smooth. The complexity was astounding, with every flavour in perfect harmony. Pure elegance in a glass.

In the heart of Italy, at 23, I went on a journey that would forever shape my relationship with wine. Surrounded by the sun-kissed vineyards of Tuscany, each tasting session felt like a revelation, a symphony of flavours unfolding on my palate. Guided by passionate experts, I explored the nuances of Italian viticulture, discovering the soul of each bottle in every sip, a sensory adventure that left a mark on my appreciation for the art of wine.

I granted the server permission to top up our glasses. After pouring the wine into our glasses, he placed the bottle in the holder by the side of the table and left. Mike held up his glass, to raise a toast, hoping to move past the question that I threw at him just before the server interrupted us. I decided to humour him.

"Here's to the nights we'll never remember with the people that we'll never forget." Now it was time to steer the conversation back to the awkward moment. I offered a toast in exchange of his. "Well, I can do you one better. Here's to the night we'll forever remember and the wife we'll pretend to forget." Mike awkwardly clinked his glass with mine and took a sip. I let him have a moment. He played with his glass for a moment and then looked up at me.

"How did you know?" he asked.

"The easiest thing to do is take off a ring, but to hide a tan line, that's a whole different skill set."

He noticed the tan line on his ring finger. He slowly slid his hand off the table and put it out of sight. I could see that he was embarrassed. It didn't really bother me that he was married.

"You don't have to be embarrassed. I noticed it on the plane."

Mike seemed slightly relieved considering I knew about it before his initiation into the mile-high club. He had done a pretty good job at keeping his private life private despite being a public personality.

"You've done well at keeping your life private, must make having affairs a lot easier right?" I said jokingly.

"Affairs? What makes you think that I've engaged in extracurricular activities like this before?" he asked defensively.

Men! They find it so hard to accept the truth. No wonder his book is called Life: Beyond Reality. He seemed to like to live in that state of mind.

"You gave in too quickly. If this was your first time you would've taken longer to follow me into the bathroom." I said with a flirty smile.

"But you're sure that I would have either way?" he asked.

"I'm all about modesty but I also know what I look like. Getting someone into bed is easy. The hard part is finding someone worth more."

Mike was intrigued. "You think I'm worth more?" he asked hopefully.

"I don't know yet. The wife holds you back by a few points, but never say never."

We spent the next hour immersed in conversation, discussing life, love, and everything in between as we savoured our meal. We indulged in the signature 'Duck & Waffle' and a portion of grilled octopus with ratte potatoes, chimichurri, and cayenne. For dessert, we went with the server's recommendation – Torrejas, though I had already enjoyed a round of dessert while Mike was on the phone with his agent earlier. Mike shared his ambition to write a thriller for his next book. Self-help was really never his passion, but it was a smart move at the time. Now, with publishers clamouring for his work, he had the freedom to explore what truly excited him. I noticed that Mike loved to talk about himself. Most women might find that annoying, but not me. I'm not particularly keen on discussing my own life, so its suited me just fine. The less they know about me the more interested they are to find out.

"I hope the meal was satisfactory?" asked the server as he presented Mike with the bill. "Everything was perfect, especially the dessert." Mike glanced over at me and winked. I'm not usually a fan of guys winking, but there was something cute about the way Mike did it. Before I could offer to pay half, Mike handed over his card to the waiter. He punched in his pin without even looking at the machine, his eyes fixed on me. The waiter returned his card along with the receipt.

"Have a lovely evening," he said, making his way back to towards the kitchen. Mike got up and offered me his hand. A true gentleman. Just as I was about to take his hand, I noticed a man walking up to us with purpose in his stride. He looked like a product of Idris Elba, having a baby with Idris Elba, to produce another Idris Elba. I guess the easier way to say it would be - a young Idris Elba. Mike noticed me staring beyond him. Just as he turned to follow my gaze, the bodacious man punched Mike right across the face, sending him crashing to the ground, right at my feet. The man looked down at Mike.

"You thought you'd just sleep with my wife and get away with it?"

Mike looked thoroughly confused. He glanced beyond Idris into the distance, where a very attractive woman was seated a few tables away – let's call her Halle Berry. Mike shyly and awkwardly waved at Halle, who waved back, trying to hide her embarrassment. Mike turned back to the man towering over him.

"How come she gets off the hook? She's the one who's committed to you. Not me"

The man took a step forward and leaned closer to Mike. He looked like he was about to punch him in the face again. "Don't push me boy, I'll clock you again. Stay the fuck away from my wife or next time... I won't be so nice." He pierced through Mike's heart with a cold stare. Mike raised his hands into the air. Idris held the stare for about 2.3 seconds before storming off with Halle. I stretched my hand out and offered it to Mike. I helped him back to his feet.

"You live quite an eventful life. I was almost expecting this to turn into a brawl." I pulled him up to his feet. He started to adjust his jacket, which had fallen off one shoulder thanks to that shattering punch.

"I'm a lover, not a fighter," he said with a smirk.

I wrapped my arm around his as we made our way out of the restaurant, as the other people stared at us in. "Good to know. I much prefer lovers," I teased, glancing at him with a playful smile. "Though, I have to admit, you do look pretty sexy taking a punch."

He chuckled, his eyes sparkling with amusement. "Well, if it impresses you, maybe it was worth it."

"Maybe," I said, leaning closer. "But let's try to avoid any more punches tonight, unless you're into that sort for thing." Now it was my turn to wink.

VII

MIKE

A bag of frozen peas rested on my left eye offering a little relief to the throbbing in my face. Natasha's Airbnb was a beautiful townhouse in the heart of Notting hill. I was laid out on the world's most comfortable couch, with a large print of a speed boat zipping through the Thames framed behind me. A cozy fireplace was nestled under the large TV screen, with the night lights streaming through the floor-to-ceiling windows. To my left, by the front door of the house was a cozy breakfast table for two, beyond which was the lavish white 8-seater dining table.

The quick tour Natasha gave me of the four bedrooms upstairs included a peek at the master bathroom, complete with a hot tub that I was sure we would use later. The master bedroom itself was a dream, with glass doors along one wall that opened out into a beautiful outdoor seating area. As I lay there on the couch, surrounded by this elegance, I couldn't help but marvel at the comfort and charm of her place, even with the dull ache in my face reminding me of the night's unexpected excitement.

I heard a beep coming from near the bookshelf. My eyes followed the sound – well, technically, just one eye since the other was covered with a bag of peas. I noticed a blue light flashing on a small Marshall speaker nestled between two piles of books. A song began to play. Within the first few notes, I knew exactly which song it was. I still remember the first time I heard it. It was back in 2007 when Tarantino's movie Death Proof hit the cinemas. Every single guy I knew back then fell in love with Vanessa Ferlito after watching her perform that lap dance for Kurt Russel in the pub scene.

I have a vivid memory of the outfit she wore in the song. It was a masterclass in understated allure, the kind that didn't just demand attention – it commanded it. She wore a sung, white T-shirt that hugged her curves in all the right places, printed with "San Francisco" and a stylized image of the Golden Gate Bridge. Her choice of shorts only added to the appeal – tight, well-word grey shorts that clung to her hips, accentuating the sway of her walk. Every time that I hear "Down in Mexico" by The Coasters I can't help but play that visual in my head, however, that image was about to change. A scar that would linger on till the end of my days.

Natasha appeared in the doorway, dressed in a full black latex outfit. The zipper was halfway down revealing just enough cleavage to make me move the bag of peas to get a better view.

"Now I see why your friends call you Black Widow," I said with a smirk on my face.

She slowly started walking in my direction, seductively, and to the beat. She walked right up to me, straddled me on the couch and brought her face so close to mine that I could feel her breath on my skin. She could feel my excitement.

"Someone seems to be in a hurry," she said.

"Now that I'm seeing the outfit up close, it seems like a logistical nightmare to get it off."

She moved past my face and whispered into my ear. "Don't worry about the logistics, I'll get it off fast enough when I need to."

She kissed me full on the mouth, a sudden, passionate force that sent a jolt through me. Her hands grabbed my shirt, and with one swift motion, she ripped the buttons apart, exposing my chest and abs. Slowly, sensually, she got off me and grabbed me by my open shirt as the song continued to play.

Natasha led me into the bedroom, her touch electrifying. She started to put on a show that made me forget all about Vanessa Ferlito. She pushed me onto the bed and began to dance around me, her movements mesmerizing. Natasha lifted one leg and placed it on my chest, gently pushing me back until I was flat out on the bed.

She climbed on top of me, her presence overwhelming. Her hand caressed my cheek, then slowly slid down my chest, leaving scratch marks with her nails that sent shivers down my spine. Leaning forward, she removed my shirt and tossed it aside. Her eyes locked onto mine, and the world outside faded away.

With a tantalizing smile, Natasha reached for the zipper and began to undo her latex suit, swiftly but sensually. The sound of the zipper echoed in the room, each inch revealing more of her smooth, flawless skin. She slid out of the suit with practiced ease, the material clinging to her curves before finally falling away. The sight of her, now fully exposed, took my breath away.

She leaned in, her breath warm against my skin, and kissed me again, deeper this time. Her hands explored my chest and abs, fingers tracing every muscle. I could feel the heat between us rising, the intensity building with every touch. Natasha's lips moved down my neck, leaving a trail of soft kisses that made my heart race. She paused, her mouth hovering over my skin, teasing me before continuing her descent.

As she moved lower, her hands followed, caressing, and exploring. She reached the waistband of my pants, her fingers deftly unbuttoning and unzipping them. I lifted my hips slightly. Helping her as she slid them off, leaving me exposed and vulnerable beneath her. She took a moment to look at me, her eyes filled with desire, before she resumed her sensual assault.

She lowered herself onto me, her body pressing against mine, skin to skin. The sensation was almost overwhelming, a mix of pleasure and anticipation. She moved slowly at first, her hips rocking gently against mine, her breath quickening. I could feel her heat as she grinded against me, our bodies moving in perfect harmony.

Her pace quickened; her movements more urgent as the music built to a crescendo. I matched her rhythm, our bodies moving together in a dance of pure ecstasy. The pleasure was intense, each thrust bringing us closer to the edge. Natasha's moans mixed with mine, the sound of passion filling the room.

Finally, the tension broke, a wave of euphoria crashing over us as we reach our climax together. Our bodies trembled with the release, the pleasure washing over us in waves. Natasha collapsed onto me, her breath ragged, her body still trembling from the intensity of our encounter.

We lay there for a moment, basking in the afterglow, our bodies entwined. Natasha's head rested on my chest, her fingers tracing lazy circles on my skin. I could feel the beat of her heart, the rhythm matching my own. I used to believe that people only orgasm together in the movies, but I don't any more.

VIII
NATASHA

I stood in the doorway, two glasses of water in my hand, staring at Mike. He looked even better with his shirt off. Mike's shirt hung loose on my body, not covering much given that the buttons had all been ripped off – by me. I walked over to him and handed him one of the glasses.

"Hydrate. You'll need it for round two," I said with a flirty smile. Mike smiled back at me and took a sip of the water. It was quite a sight – two half naked people, half under the covers, lying next to each other, sipping on water. I turned to look at Mike.

"Do you believe in Karma?" I asked.

One eyebrow went higher than the other, just like on the flight. "That came out of nowhere... What kind of question is that?" He placed his glass on the side table and turned completely towards me.

"A simple one. Let me repeat. Do you believe in Karma?" I said again.

"Sure," he replied.

"No but do you really believe in Karma or are you just humouring me?" I asked, eager to know his view on the subject.

He paused, looking deeply into my eyes. "I believe in karma," he responded, his voice sincere.

Before Mike could say another word, I tossed the water from my glass right in his face.

"What the fuck? Why did you do that?" he spluttered, wiping the water from his eyes.

"How do you feel right now? At this very moment?" I asked, my tone calm.

"Like I want to pick up my glass and throw the water in your face. See how you like that."

"See? Revenge. Not karma. A lot of people say they believe in karma, but their actions and intentions speak otherwise."

Mike looked at me, bewildered. "I consider myself a fairly intelligent member of the species, but this my dear, makes no sense."

"If you truly believed in karma, then you wouldn't care that I just threw water in your face. You would let karma handle it. The fact that you're feeling the need to exact revenge means you don't really believe in karma."

Mike had a semi-jaw drop moment. He was processing my words, and I could see the gears turning in his head. But what was bothering him more was that he, an intelligent member of the species, wasn't able to come to that conclusion himself. Oh, the male ego. Such a fragile thing, isn't it?

SPLASH!

Out of nowhere, Mike threw the water from his glass right back at me. I respond with a playful slap across his face. He screamed in a high-pitched voice.

"Aaaah! What the fuck! What happened to Karma?"

I smirked. "I never said that I believe in it."

And it's true. I've never believed in Karma – not the way most people do, anyway. The idea that the universe will somehow balance out all the good and bad on its own seems like a lazy excuse for inaction. In my world, you don't wait for Karma to catch up; you create your own. If you want something, you have to make it happen, not sit around hoping the universe will drop it in your lap. The world doesn't turn on its own; it needs a push, a nudge in the right direction. And that push comes from being smart, strategic, and unafraid to take what's yours. Good things come to those who don't wait but who make their own luck, bending the world to fit their desires. That's the real Karma. That's what I'm chasing.

Mike slowly caressed his face, trying to soothe the sting. "I'm going to consider that as foreplay then."

And with that, he pounced on top of me, ready to begin round two. The night outside our window carried on, indifferent to the fiery exchange unfolding inside.

IX

NATASHA

I opened the front door and stepped out with Mike right behind me, holding my hand. We were dressed for a new day. 'I put a spell on you' by Annie Lennox played in my head. We walked through the streets, stealing glances at each other, our smiles reflecting the night's passion.

We found ourselves sitting in a cozy coffee shop. Mike had his arm around me, and we were sitting on the same side of the table like a couple who can't bear to sit apart. He took a bite of a pain au chocolat, and a trail of the chocolate oozed from the corner of his lip down to his chin. I scooped it up with my finger and slowly stuck my finger in my mouth, ensuring not to leave any chocolate behind. Mike had that 'Life Beyond Reality' look on his face. I stared at him seductively and then shifted my gaze to the bathroom door at the far end of the café. He followed my look and noticed the door too.

The door clicked shut behind us, the soft hum of the café fading into the background. The bathroom was small, but not as small as the one on the flight. I pushed Mike against the tiled wall, pressing my body against his, my lips finding his in a feverish kiss. His hands roamed my back, pulling me even closer. I broke the kiss, our breaths mingling as I whispered, "This seems familiar."

With a mischievous smile, I unbuttoned his jeans, my fingers grazing his skin, eliciting a sharp intake of breath from him. His hands slipped under my dress, hiking it up and revealing my Agent Provocateur underwear. His lips found my neck, leaving a trail of hot, lingering kisses as he lifted me up effortlessly, pinning me against the cool bathroom wall.

My legs wrapped around his waist, my dress riding up as we lost ourselves in the moment. The sensation of his body pressed against mine was electric, each touch sending shivers down my spine. Our breaths became ragged, mingling in the heated air between us. His fingers dug into my thighs as he supported my weight, our bodies moving together in a perfect, primal rhythm.

The small bathroom echoed with our gasps and whispers, the sound of our passion filling the space. It was raw, intense, and utterly consuming. Every thrust drove us closer to the edge, our connection deepening with every movement. As we reached the peak of our shared ecstasy, I bit my lip to stifle a moan, my fingers tangling in his hair as I buried my face in his shoulder, feeling the world blur around us.

Afterwards, we stayed there for a moment, catching our breath, the reality of our surroundings slowly coming back. I smoothed down my dress and fixed my hair, giving him a playful smirk. "Ready for coffee now?" I asked, my voice still a little breathless. He chuckled, nodding, and we step back into the café, the secrecy of our encounter adding a thrilling edge to our coffee date.

After an exhilarating coffee date, we ended up in an even more thrilling lingerie store. The air in the store was filled with a subtle scent of vanilla and the soft rustle of the luxurious fabrics. Mike sat down in the plush velvet chair placed just outside the fitting rooms, his eyes following me as I disappeared behind the curtain.

The first set I tried on was a sleek, black lace ensemble that clung to my body in all the right places. I yanked the curtain open, revealing myself to Mike. His jaw dropped, eyes widening with appreciation. The song by Annie Lennox was now playing on my phone as I put on a show for him. I stepped out, giving him a full view, and did a slow turn to the beat, letting him admire every angle. His gaze was intense, devouring every inch of me. I could feel his desire growing, mirroring my own.

Next, I tried on a red satin number with delicate lace trim. The fabric felt cool against my skin, and as I opened the curtain, Mike's eyes lit up even more. I walked towards him, stopping just inches away, letting him drink in the sight. His hands twitched, wanting to reach out, but he stayed put, savouring the visual feast.

I returned behind the curtain, slipping into a playful pink set with intricate embroidery. The sheer material left little to the imagination. When I stepped out this time, Mike's reaction was even more pronounced. He leaned forward, his lips parting slightly as he took me in. I turned and headed back behind the curtain, giving him one last teasing look over my shoulder. "Enjoying the show?" I asked with a playful smile.

"More than you can imagine," he replied, his voice husky with need.

I modelled a few more stunning lingerie sets for Mike, each one more provocative than the last. He sat back, enjoying his private Victoria's Secret fashion show, his eyes never leaving me. The connection between us was palpable, the air thick with unspoken promises.

As the last notes of 'I put a spell on you' played, I stepped out one final time, wearing the first black lace set. I walked up to Mike, straddling his lap, leaning in close, whispering in his ear, "Let's take this somewhere more private."

He nodded, his hands resting on my hips, ready to follow my lead. Together, we left the store, our hearts racing with anticipation for what's to come.

We arrived at the apartment, slightly drunk, our lips locked in a heated kiss as we stumbled through the door. Our hands were everywhere, clothes being discarded along the way. By the time we reached the kitchen, I was left in the black lace set that clung to my body, while Mike stood completely naked, his eyes dark with desire.

The island counter in the centre of the kitchen became our playground. With a mischievous grin, Mike grabbed me by the waist and lifted me onto the counter. I leaned back, my hands resting on the slightly elevated section behind me. My fingers slid across the smooth surface, and a bottle of olive oil caught a nudge from my elbow, nosediving to the wooden floor below. The oil spilt out, slowly spreading across the floor, but was quickly forgotten as our moans filled the room.

Mike stepped between my legs, his hands gliding up my thighs, spreading them wider as he pressed his body against mine. His lips found mine again, our tongues dancing in a fiery kiss. He trailed kisses down my neck, sucking and nibbling, leaving a path of heat in his wake. His hands explored every inch of my body, caressing, squeezing, and teasing through the delicate lace.

I arched my back, my breath hitching as his mouth found the sensitive skin of my chest. His hand slipped under the waistband of my panties, his fingers brushing against my most intimate area. The sensation was electric, making me gasp and writhe against him. He slipped one finger inside, then two, moving with expert precision.

I gripped the counter behind me, my fingers digging into the surface as I lifted my hips to meet his touch. The intensity built between us, every touch, every kiss driving us closer to the edge. He withdrew his fingers, and I whimpered at the loss, but he quickly replaced them with his hard length, entering me with a slow, deliberate thrust.

The world narrowed down to the feeling of him inside me, the way our bodies moved together in perfect sync. The counter beneath me was cool against my skin, a stark contrast to the heat building between us. Our movements became more urgent, our breaths coming in short, ragged gasps.

His hands gripped my hips, pulling me closer, deeper. My legs wrapped around his waist, heels digging into his back as I clung to him. The kitchen filled with the sounds of our passion, the rhythmic sounds of our bodies moving together, mingled with our gasps and whispers.

As we climbed higher, the tension coiled tighter within me. Mike's eyes locked onto mine, and the intensity in his gaze pushed me closer to the edge. With a final, deep thrust, we both shattered, our cries of ecstasy echoing through the apartment.

I buried my face in his shoulder, my body trembling with the aftershock of our release. He held me close, his breath hot against my ear, as we came down from the high together. The spilled olive oil was a forgotten puddle on the floor, a testament to the passion we unleashed in the heat of the moment.

X

MIKE

That had been the best weekend of my life, hands down. I'd never felt so alive, so connected, and as I sat on the edge of the bed, dressed in jeans and a black t-shirt, I couldn't shake the sadness that it was all coming to an end, but every dream ends in reality, and so must this. My black sports jacket lay next to me, and my stroller stood tall, ready for the journey back home. If the story had ended here, where it was meant to, the things about to happen, never would have and life, would have been different.

"The car should be here in a few minutes," I said, trying to sound casual.

Natasha, dressed in her bathrobe, looked at me with a soft smile. "Hope you've had a good weekend."

"It's been surreal," I replied, and it was true. Every moment with her had been extraordinary.

"So, this is it, huh? The end?" I asked, my voice tinged with reluctance.

"If that's how you want to look at it. I'd rather say... Until we meet again," she responded with a hopeful glint in her eyes.

"You think we will?" I asked, needing to hear her say yes.

"I spend more than half the year in Bombay. It's a big city, but it's not that big, "she said, her smile reassuring. "But honestly, it all depends on you Mike. You have a wife, and I'm single. It's up to you how this plays out," she said, her eyes locking onto mine with a mix of sincerity and challenge.

I felt a pang of guilt, but also a deep, undeniable connection. "Certain connections are so strong that nothing can keep them apart," I said, trying to convince myself of the possibility of an alternate reality. Humans weren't built for monogamy, but it's the acceptance that we struggle with.

She smiled again, and I couldn't help but laugh a little. "You know it's funny..."

"What is?" she asked.

"In the two days that we've spend together, I know every curve on your body, every birthmark, every wrinkle... But there's one very important thing about you that I don't know," I said, looking into her eyes.

"Firstly, I don't have any wrinkles," she retorted with a playful smirk. "What don't you know?"

"What do you do?" I asked, genuinely curious. "What do you do for a living? Do you work? Do you have family money? Do you sell drugs? Are you and undercover police officer?"

"Undercover police officer? Wow, a writer's brain is such an intriguing thing," she laughed. "I'm a dancer."

"Wow! I guess that makes sense given the way you move. What kind of dancer?" I press, intrigued.

"Exotic," she replied simply.

I paused, absorbing this new piece of information. "Exotic?" I repeated, letting the word hang in the air between us. "How did you end up being an exotic dancer?"

She met my gaze, her eyes steady and unwavering. "Because I'm good at it," she said confidently. "I always loved dancing so why not? The money is great, and I get to be my own boss. How many people can actually say that they do what they love for a living?"

I nodded slowly, considering her words. There was a sincerity in her voice that was hard to ignore. "I guess not many people can say that," I admitted. "It's just… fascinating. You seem so comfortable with it."

She shrugged, a faint smile playing on her lips. "It's my choice. I enjoy it. It gives me freedom and independence and makes me feel seen. And it's not just about the money or the performance. It's about owning who I am and what I do."

I couldn't help but admire her confidence and self-assurance. "That's incredible," I said, genuinely impressed. "I think it's amazing that you've found something you love and made it your own."

She leaned in, her eyes sparkling with amusement. "Thank you, Mike. Not everyone understands, but it's nice to be appreciated."

"But what is it that you do in Bombay for half the year?" I asked, still curious.

"Same job, different audience," she said nonchalantly.

"Really? Is it safe?" I asked, concerned.

"I only do private dances with very elite, verified clients. Celebrities, business owners, the kind of crowd that can't afford to cause much trouble."

"I would have expected the exact opposite," I admitted.

"Are you a fan of the Avengers?" she asked, seemingly out of nowhere.

"Eh! A tad," I responded, puzzled.

"If the Hulk were standing in front of you, would you fuck with him?" she asked, a mischievous glint in her eyes.

"The Hulk? That freakishly large green guy? No way! I'd run as far away as I could," I laughed.

"That's what my bouncer looks like, just less green," she said, joining in the laughter.

Just then, my phone rang, as if on cue. I answered it. "Hello? I'll be right out," I said, hanging up. "I guess it's time."

Natasha walked up to me and planted a big kiss right on my mouth. "Until we meet again Mr. Writer?" she whispered.

"Until we meet again," I replied, pulling her close one last time before I had to go.

XI

MIKE

The vibrancy of Bombay envelops me once more. Gone are the iconic black taxi, the red buses, and the sensuality and charm of Natasha. The romantic escape I left behind has been replaced by the relentless energy and chaos of my reality.

The small digital clock on my work desk, in my home office, shows the time – 2:45 a.m. I'm seated in my study, typing away furiously on my laptop. Every keystroke is an attempt to relive the memories of my weekend encounter with Natasha. It's been almost a week since I've been back, but it feels like it was only yesterday that we were wrapped in each other's arms making naked poetry together. Her image, her touch, her voice – everything about her is etched into my mind. Every fifteen keystrokes, I hear a moan from Natasha, and every twenty-five, I see a flash of our passionate moments together. It's as if she's still here with me, haunting my thoughts and my words.

It's becoming clear that my next book will revolve around this torrid love affair. So much for writing a thriller.

"Honey!"

I stop typing and turn towards the sound of the voice. In the doorway of the room stands Natasha, dressed in a provocative white negligee. My heart skips a beat.

"Aren't you coming to bed?" she asks.

I blink a couple of times and look back at the door. It's not Natasha. It's a different woman. The negligee is the same, though. An attractive woman. Maybe not as striking as Natahsa, but attractive enough to hold a man down for one lifetime, or maybe even a lifetime and half. This is Rhea, my wife. Her dark hair cascades down in soft waves, framing a face that once captivated me. Her dark eyes, full of depth and warmth, hold my gaze but are unable to erase the memory of Natasha. Her smile – it's radiant and genuine, reminiscent of Jessica Alba's, lighting up her entire face and yet, all I see is Natasha.

"You've been cooped up in this room since you got back. I thought you might need some R&R," she says.

My head is racing with visions of me and Natahsa. The intensity of our connection, the passion we shared – it's all-consuming. I take a moment to decide. I don't want Rhea to wonder why I'm acting distant. We've been married almost 5 years now and she knows the inspiration to write never outweighs her dressed in an outfit like that. I slam the laptop shut and lift Rhea, carrying her to our bedroom. I throw her down on the bed, my mind flickering between reality and the intoxicating memories of Natahsa.

As I hover over Rhea, her features blur and morph into Natasha's face. I kiss her deeply, but it's Natasha's lips I feel. Rhea moans softly beneath me, yet it's Natasha's voice that echoes in my ears. My hands trace the familiar curves of Rhea's body, but my mind replaces each sensation with memories of Natasha.

Rhea's hands run through my hair, pulling me closer. I try to stay present, to focus on her, but Natasha's image is too powerful. Her scent, her touch, the way her eyes looked into mine – it all floods back, overwhelming my senses. Rhea's body responds eagerly to my touch, but in my mind, it's Natasha I'm caressing, Natasha I'm loving.

As I undress Rhea, her body writhes beneath my hands, her skin warm and inviting. But every touch, every kiss, is a memory of Natahsa. I slide my hands down her sides, feeling the familiar curve of her hips, but it's Natasha's body that my fingers remember. I kiss Rhea's neck, her shoulders, but it's Natasha's taste I crave.

Rhea pulls me closer, her nails digging into my back as she whispers my name. I respond to her, but my mind is miles away, lost in the echoes of Natasha's moans. The way Natasha arched her back, the softness of her sighs, the intensity of her desire – it's all replaying in my mind guiding my movements with Rhea.

Our bodies move together in a rhythm that feels almost mechanical. I'm present in the moment, but my heart isn't here. With each thrust, I see Natasha beneath me, hear her gasping for breath, feel her fingers clawing at my back. I feel a pang of guilt. The memory is so vivid that it overshadows the reality of Rhea's body beneath mine.

As the guilt becomes unbearable, I can't shake the feeling that I'm betraying Rhea with every thought of Natasha. Desperation claws at me, and I turn Rhea around, guiding her to face away from me. It's a cowardly move, but I can't bear to look into her eyes any longer, those eyes that trust and love me without question. I make love to her from behind, our bodies still moving together, but now it's easier to let my mind wander, to pretend it's Natasha in my arms. The mechanical rhythm continues, but now it's devoid of any lingering pretence of intimacy. Rhea's soft moans reach my ears, but still, all I hear are the echoes of Natasha's sighs. I close my eyes, trying to focus on the present, but the weight of my guilt presses down, suffocating any true connection between us.

Twenty-three minutes later...

I lie in bed, breathing heavily, looking at Rhea. By the look on my face, you can tell I'm not really looking at her, but rather, looking beyond her. Guilt gnaws at me, but the pull of my memories is stronger.

"You've come back a new man... I like it," Rhea says, her voice a contented purr.

I smile, thankful that I was able to play my part of the devoted husband well enough.

A few hours later. I'm lying in bed, wide awake. Beside me, Rhea is sleeping like a baby. I can't get Natasha out of my head. The weekend we spent together was more than just an affair; it was a revelation. I roll a little to my side, about sixteen degrees, and reach for my phone on the bedside table. I start typing a message while looking over to re-confirm that Rhea is still deep in her slumber. I hit send. A decision I would soon come to regret more than anything else in my life.

MIKE: When are you back? I can't stop thinking about you.

Moments later, my phone vibrates. Luckily, I was smart enough to turn off the ringer. Natasha responds.

NATASHA: This morning.

MIKE: Can I see you again?

NATASHA: I have no reason to say no.

The thought of seeing Natasha again ignites a thrill in me that I can't ignore. The pull towards her is undeniable, and as much as I try to anchor myself in the life I've built here, the allure of what we shared is too strong. My heart races with anticipation for our next encounter, even as I lie next to my sleeping wife.

XII

RHEA

The morning sunlight streamed through the curtains, casting a warm glow over our bedroom. I wake up feeling refreshed, the memory of last night lingering in my mind. Mike's touch, his intensity – it's as if he has been reborn. I turn to look at him, still sound asleep, his chest rising and falling with each breath. A smile creeps onto my lips. He looks peaceful, content, and utterly irresistible. Sometimes I wonder how I ever got so lucky to end up with someone as perfect as him.

Our night together had been incredible, a beautiful reminder of the deep connection we share. There's a renewed passion in him that I haven't seen in years. Since he returned from London, he seems different, more alive. As an artist, I understand the ebbs and flows of inspiration, and I'm thrilled that he has found his muse again.

I slip out of bed, careful not to wake him, and make my way to the kitchen. The aroma of fresh coffee soon fills the air, and I pour myself a cup, savouring the warmth. As I take a sip, I let my mind wander back to how we first met.

It was at my first art exhibition, a night that felt almost magical. The gallery was buzzing with people, but it was Mike who caught my eye. He stood in front of one of my paintings, lost in thought. His eyes reflected a depth and understanding that immediately drew me in.

"What do you see?" I asked, curious about his perspective.

He turned to me, his face lighting up with a smile. "A life beyond reality," he said, his voice smooth and captivating.

I laughed, delighted by his response. "That would make a great title for a book."

His eyes sparkled with interest. "You think so? Maybe I'll use it."

"You're a writer? I asked intrigued.

"Unpublished though, but hopefully not for long."

"Here's to hope," I said, extending my hand. "I'm Rhea."

"Mike," he said, taking my hand in his. There was an instant connection, a spark that was undeniable. We spent the rest of the evening talking, our conversation flowing effortlessly. By the end of the night, I knew I had met someone special.

Since then, our lives had intertwined in the most beautiful ways. We had supported each other through every high and low. The book Mike was writing back then never made it to the stands but when Covid hit, he found inspiration and ended up writing a best-selling novel called 'Life: Beyond Reality.' After its success though, Mike had been struggling, he seemed lost. The inspiration that once flowed so freely had dried up. I watched him battle with his frustration, feeling helpless but hopeful. Being an artist myself, I could relate to his struggle. Fortunately, thanks to the success of 'Life: Beyond Reality' we were able to live a rather lavish life.

Then came his trip to London. He went to receive a Baillie Gifford Prize for his book, a well-deserved recognition for his work. But something else happened on that trip. He came back a changed man. There was a spark in his eyes, a renewed vigour in his step. It was as if the award had reignited a fire within him.

I'm brought back to the present by the sound of footsteps. I turn to see Mike standing in the doorway, looking at me with that familiar, loving gaze.

"Good morning," he says, his voice husky from sleep.

"Good morning my love," I reply, walking over to him and wrapping my arms around his waist. "Did you sleep well?"

He nods, pulling me close. "I did. Last night was…"

"Incredible," I say with a smile, feeling a warmth spread though me. "You seem different, more passionate. It's like you've found your muse again."

He kisses the top of my head, holding me tightly. "I have. London was… transformative. I feel inspired again, like I have so much more to write."

I look up at him, my eyes filled with admiration. "I'm so happy to hear that. I've missed seeing you like this."

He cups my face in his hands, his eyes searching mine. "Thank you for always believing in me, Rhea. You're my anchor, my constant."

I feel a lump in my throat, overwhelmed by the love I feel for this man. "And you're my everything Mike."

We stand there for a moment, wrapped in each other's arms, savouring the intimacy of the morning. Eventually, he goes into his writing den, where he sits at his laptop and starts typing away, a look of determination on his face.

As I watch him work, I can't help but feel a surge of pride. This is the man I fell in love with, the man who captured my heart with his words and his passion. He's back, and I know that whatever comes next, we will face it together.

"I'm going to hop in for a quick shower and then head down to the studio. Would you like to join me in the shower?" I say hoping for a replay of last night.

He looks up at me with a smile on his face. "There's nothing I would love more, but you know how it is, when inspiration hits..."

"I know. I'll leave you to it," I say, shutting the door as I make my way to the bathroom.

As I work on my new collection, I can't help but feel grateful for the life that I have with Mike. I know the world is full of surprises and challenges, but with Mike by my side, there's nothing we can't handle. We have each other, and that is more than enough.

XIII

MIKE

As the front door clicks shut behind Rhea, a wave of relief washes over me. Her departure for work feels like the first breath of air after being submerged too long. The guilt gnaws at my insides, a relentless reminder of the deceit I carry. Pretending to be the devoted husband, smiling, and playing the part, has been exhausting. Every touch, every kiss with Rhea has felt like a betrayal to both her and Natasha. I sink into the couch, head in hands, torn between the comfort of familiarity and the pull of forbidden excitement. I can't deny it any longer; I'm desperate to see Natasha again. The thought of her electrifies me, making it impossible to focus on anything else. She's got me writing again, something that I had almost forgotten how to do. I pick up my phone from the table and make the call.

Natasha's house sits quaintly on Carter Road, a charming anomaly amid the towering apartment complexes that flank it. This small sea-facing bungalow has an unassuming elegance, with its whitewashed walls and a red-tiled roof that hints at old-world charm. Large, lush potted plants frame the entrance, and the salty sea breeze rustles through the leaves. However, the once breathtaking view of the sea is now marred by the sprawling construction site for the new sea bridge. The serene horizon is cluttered with cranes, the incessant hum of machinery filling the air. It's a stark contrast to the tranquillity Natasha's home exudes, a daily reminder of the city's relentless march towards modernization. From the front, the panoramic view of the sea is still there, but now it shares space with the chaotic progress of urban development.

It's a ten-minute drive from my house, yet it feels like a world apart. Every morning, I lace up my running shoes and hit the pavement of Cater Road, my regular route skirting past her bungalow. Despite the proximity, I've never once crossed paths with Natasha during these runs. It's almost as if fate had kept our encounter confined to a more intimate setting.

The afternoon sun filters through the thin curtains, casting a soft glow on Natasha's bedroom. We're tangled in the sheets, the scent of our recent passion lingering in the air. I run my fingers through my hair, savouring the moment.

"Who said sex needs to be a nighttime event?" I muse, my eyes tracing the contours of her body, more vivid in the daylight. "I get to see so much more of you in the sunlight. Beautiful."

Natasha chuckles softly, her eyes glinting with amusement. "Ah, the philosophy of daylight love. Who knew you were such a profound thinker?"

I smirk, glancing at my watch, noting the time. "I still have an hour before I need to go. Round two?"

"You don't have to ask me twice," she purrs, climbing on top of me and pressing her lips to mine. Her kiss is electrifying, igniting a fresh wave of desire.

Her hands glide over my chest, and I can't help but marvel at the intensity of our connection. The world outside the window fades as we lose ourselves in each other once again, the daylight making every touch, every kiss more vivid and real. Her movements are both deliberate and wild, a tantalizing dance of passion that leaves us both breathless. The room fills with the sounds of our fervour, each gasp and moan heightening the pleasure. As she arches her back, her eyes locked onto mine, I know this is a moment I'll replay in my mind again and again.

Back in my dimly lit study, the memory of Natasha's touch fuels my creative frenzy. My fingers fly over the keyboard, capturing the heat and passion of our encounters in words. This book is turning out to be one of the spiciest stories I've ever written, each keystroke echoing the intensity of our affair.

Earlier, Rhea had poked her head into the room, her voice soft and inviting. "Mike, come to bed. It's late, and you need some rest."

I had looked up from my laptop, seeing the concern in her eyes, and she added, "How's the book coming along? Can I get a sneak peek?"

I smiled at her, shaking my head gently. "You know the system, Rhea. You read it only when it's ready."

She had nodded, giving me a small smile before retreating, leaving me alone with my inspiration and my guilt.

My phone buzzes on the desk, the screen lighting up with 'Agent calling.' For a moment, I hesitate. The pressure from the publishers has been mounting. I took an advance almost a year ago, right after the release of 'Life Beyond Reality,' and I haven't shown them anything yet. Money has been tight and so far, I've been able to keep Rhea from knowing the truth. I was worried at some point, the anxiety gnawing at me as I struggled to find my next big idea. But now, with my new found inspiration, I know I've struck gold. The world is always ravenous for a well-crafted tale of desire. There's an insatiable hunger for words that ignite the imagination and stir the deepest passions. I've tapped into that primal need thanks to my exploits with Natasha. People can't get enough of a story that makes their pulse quicken and their breath catch. It's not just writing; it's seduction on the page.

I stare at my phone a little longer before answering. "Mike," Ashish's voice comes through the phone, heavy with concern. "We've got a situation. The publishers are breathing down my neck. They were already pissed off that you ditched the Baillie Gifford Prize event and now they're threatening to dissolve the contract if they don't see some pages soon."

"Fuck! Seriously?" I lean back, pinching the bridge of my nose. "I just need a little more time. I'm onto something big, I swear."

"How many pages do you have so far?" he asks, sounding more stressed than usual.

"Twenty-three," I admit, wincing a little at how small that number sounded.

"Twenty-three? Mike, that's barely anything! You're asking for trouble. you know how these contracts work. We're already behind schedule."

"I know, I know. But this new idea... they're going to love it. I can feel it. I just need to flesh it out a bit more."

"You've been saying that for weeks. They're losing patience, and honestly, so am I. How much longer do you need?"

"Just a couple more weeks. I'm really close. I promise." I lie, trying to buy as much time as I can for now.

"A couple of weeks, Mike? That's a tough ask. They want progress now, not promises."

"I understand, but rushing it isn't going to do anyone any good. Trust me on this. Give me two weeks, and I'll have something solid to show them."

"Alright, I'll try to buy you some time. But this is it, Mike. You better pull off a miracle, or everything's going to go belly up. It's been more than a year since Life beyond reality hit the stands and if this contract is scrapped, it's going to be close to impossible to get you another deal."

"Yes, I know, Ashish. I'll get it done."

I hang up, the weight of the conversation settling on my shoulders. Two weeks. That's all the time I have. Time to dig deep and make this work.

XIV

MIKE

I stand at the entrance of the kitchen, watching as Rhea moves to the music of Miles Davis playing softly from the iPhone docked in the corner. She cracks an egg into the frying pan with practiced ease, the raw yolk landing next to another already sizzling. As she sprinkles the salt over the egg, her movements are graceful and rhythmic, perfectly in sync with the jazz. She pops two slices of bread into the toaster, a small smile playing on her lips.

"Morning!" I say as I stand there watching, all six of my abs on display. My robe is left open, and my boxers cover a small percentage of my lower body.

Rhea turns around, a smile on her face. "Did you manage to get any sleep?"

"I'll sleep when I'm dead," I reply with a grin.

"Dramatic!" she laughs, turning back to the frying pan.

I pour myself a cup of coffee and sit down. The toast pops out of the toaster, ready for consumption. Rhea places a plate in front of me with two perfectly cooked fried eggs and toast, browned to perfection. She moves back to the pan to make her own breakfast.

Ding-dong!

The doorbell rings.

"Can you please get that?" Rhea calls out.

"Sure."

Fasten your seatbelt, the turbulence is about to hit hard. I get up slowly and drag my feet to the door. Far behind me, I see a hint of Rhea in the kitchen, working on her eggs. I open the door. Nobody there. I take a step out and look around. The stairs leading down, empty. The stairs leading up to the roof, empty. The elevator, parked on 'G.' What the actual fuck? As I'm shutting the door, my eye catches something on the floor, on top of the doormat. A black envelope. I bend down and pick it up, checking both sides. There's nothing written on it. I open it. A flash drive. Again, what the fuck? Who the fuck is actually the more appropriate question of the moment.

"Who is it, honey?" Rhea yells from the kitchen.

For a moment, I contemplate whether to tell her about the envelope or not. The uncertainty troubles me, but I decide against it until I find out what's actually on the thing. "No one," I yell, walking back towards the kitchen.

"What do you mean by no one?" Rhea asks as I take my seat.

Instinctively, I use the excuse of the neighbour's kid who has actually rung the bell and run off a couple of times in the past. "Must be that asshole kid from downstairs. This isn't the first time he's rung the bell and run off. Fucking kids!"

"It's okay Mike, he's just a kid," she says, sliding the eggs from the pan to her plate.

I roll my eyes and go back to eating my breakfast. Fucking kids.

Sometime later, I'm pulling on a pair of jeans, the robe still on. Rhea enters the room and walks towards the bathroom door.

"I'm going to have a quick shower and head off to the studio. What are you up to today?' she asks.

"Write. What else is out there for me?" I reply.

"Dramatic," she says, shaking her head with a smile as she shuts the bathroom door.

I take the envelope out of the robe pocket and slide it into the pocket of my jeans. I pull out a black t-shirt from the wardrobe and put it on. Hearing the sound of Rhea turning on the shower, I quickly rush to my study and open up my laptop. I plug in the flash drive and open the folder.

A video of Natasha and me making love in her Bombay house fills the screen. Someone was filming us yesterday. Voyeuristic pornography of sorts. I feel like I've been cock-punched. I'm frozen stiff. This twist in the story was not something I was prepared for.

"Honey?" Rhea's voice calls out, startling me. I slam the laptop screen shut just as she pops her head into the study, catching the moment of impact.

"Woah! What's going on?" she asks, her eyes widening in surprise.

"Nothing... Just, one of those days..." I stammer, trying to get it together.

She seems to understand my predicament, obviously not the real one, but the one I'm pretending to be in. "There's half a fatty in the box on the coffee table... In case you need the assist."

"Thanks," I mutter.

"Also, have you seen my keys? I can't seem to find them. They aren't in my purse or on the hook by the door."

"Check your pockets from yesterday's clothes?" I suggest, my mind elsewhere.

Rhea nods and walks away. I stare at the flash drive sticking out of my laptop, quickly yanking it out and shoving it into my pocket. Stress claws at me, but can you blame me?

"Found it!" Rhea yells from the other room. A few seconds later, she reappears in the study, her face lit up with a smile. "I knew I married you for a reason."

"There are leftovers in the fridge for lunch. I'll be back in time for dinner." She blows a couple of flying kisses in my direction and walks off.

Now free to process, I get up from my chair and walk quickly to the living room. I pick up a small box from the coffee table and open it, my hands shaking. Nervous Mike isn't something I'm used to. I pull out a half-smoked joint and spark it up, taking a big drag in an attempt to calm myself down. As I exhale, I pull out my phone and start scrolling through my contacts. I dial a number, pacing up and down the living room, puffing away on the joint, waiting for Natasha to answer.

"I need to see you right away," I say urgently.

"Is everything okay, Mike? What's wrong?" Natasha's voice comes through the line, filled with concern.

"I'll explain everything when I see you. Please. When can we meet?"

"Can you come now? I'm home," she replies.

"I'll see you in fifteen," I say, taking another drag from the joint, bracing myself for what's about to come.

XV
NATASHA

I watch through the window as Mike's car pulls up across the street. He gets out, his face tense and strained. My heart sinks as I see him pacing for a moment before crossing the road and heading towards my bungalow. The knot in my stomach tightens. Whatever has brought him here can't be good.

He steps inside, his eyes meeting mine with a mix of panic and frustration. "How the fuck did this happen? He mutters under his breath, starting to pace the living room.

I walk up to him and grab him by the arm, stopping him from pacing. "Mike, calm down. What happened? What's going on?"

He looks at me, his face pale. "There's a video, Natasha. Of us. Someone filmed us when I was here yesterday. I found it on a flash drive left at my door."

I widen my eyes in shock as I let go of him. "What? Are you serious?" I ask, trying to keep my voice steady.

"If Rhea finds out about this, not only is she going to leave me, but she's also going to take me for everything I've got... And my publishers, don't even get me started on them..." He pauses, the weight of the situation settling heavily. "And this whole thing is going to turn into quite the literary scandal."

I narrow my eyes at him, the reality sinking in. "I like how you think that this only affects you. I'm in that video too. Just because I'm not married doesn't mean that I'm okay with people seeing me like that."

"It's not the same, Natsha... I mean, come on... You're a..." He stops himself just in time and walks away from me.

"... exotic dancer? Right? That's what you were going to say?" I challenge, my voice icy.

"No, of course not," he lies, turning back to look at me, and we both know it.

"Just because I dance provocatively in front of a bunch of people doesn't mean I'm okay to have my private life exposed to the public. I'm a dancer, not a Pornstar, and even Pornstar's deserve their privacy when they want it."

He pauses, looking apologetic. "I'm sorry, that was very insensitive of me."

I'm quiet, upset, and he tries to change the topic. "What I don't understand is who would do something like that and how did they even get inside to take the video?"

"Have you seen any security outside my house?" I retort.

"FUCK!" Mike explodes, his mood swinging wildly. Calm on second, and then crazy the next. "Why! Why! Why! This is so fucked up. We should have just left this whole thing behind in London."

"You called me, Mike... Not the other way around."

"Yeah, I know..." He looks defeated. "This just doesn't make any sense."

A heavy silence falls between us. Neither of us know what to make of the situation. The weight of the uncertainty presses down, making it hard to breathe.

Finally, I break the silence. "No one sends empty threats. There has to be an agenda. They obviously want something from you."

Mike's eyes narrow, a new suspicion creeping into his gaze. "Wait a minute... How do I know it wasn't you who did this?"

I freeze, the accusation hitting me like a punch to the gut. "Excuse me? Are you seriously accusing me of this?"

"Well, who else could have done it? No one else knows about us and you know where I live," he says, his voice rising.

My blood boils at the insinuation. "You've got some nerve, Mike. Why the hell would I do something like that? What would I gain from it?"

"I don't know, maybe you want something from me? Maybe you're trying to manipulate me?" His voice is harsh, filled with irrational fear and frustration.

"You really think I'm that desperate?" I snap back. "You think I'd risk everything for some sick game? I have my own life, my own career. I don't need to blackmail you to get what I want."

He pauses, looking unsure, the anger draining from his face. "I... I don't know what to think. I'm just scared, Natasha. This could ruin everything."

I step closer, my voice steady and firm. "Mike, listen to me. I didn't do this. I'm just as much a victim as you are. We need to figure out who did this and why. Blaming each other isn't going to solve anything."

He takes a deep breath, his shoulders slumping. "You're right. I'm sorry. I'm just... I don't know what to do."

"We'll figure it out," I say, softer now. "But we need to stay calm and think this through. Whoever did this has to have an agenda, and we need to find out what it is before it's too late."

"But what can we do?" he asks, desperation creeping into his voice.

"Fuck if I know... I guess we'll have to just wait and find out."

"And I'm supposed to just sit back with my dick in my hand and do nothing?" Mike snaps.

"No, God no, that's the kind of shit that got you into trouble in the first place," I retort sarcastically.

He glares at me, clearly not appreciating the humour. I sigh and try to move the conversation forward. "Do you have any idea of who it could be?"

"Is there any way to find out who came into the compound? Cameras or something?" he asks hopefully.

I shake my head. No cameras, no security.

"This is a really unsafe way to live, Natasha," he says, frustration evident.

"I'm barely ever here. The owner never bothered about security and until now, I never felt the need for it. A lock on the gate has been enough to keep me safe."

Mike falls silent, looking utterly lost. "Whoever did this will get in touch with you, they have to want something."

"What if Rhea has opened the door?" he asks, panic in his voice.

I walk up to him and hold his hands, trying to steady him. "But she didn't. Just hang in there. We'll figure this out."

He looks at me, deeply concerned. "What if they send more?"

"I think you should just get home and stay there until we hear something."

He signs, resigned. "I guess you're right."

As I watch him walk towards his car, through the window, a bitter thought crosses my mind. How ironic that the man who so willingly cheated on his wife and started an affair with me now seems hell-bent on saving his marriage. The same marriage he so easily put at risk. It's almost laughable, but the gravity of the situation keeps any trace of amusement at bay.

XVI

RHEA

I shut the door behind me as I enter the house, lost in thoughts about my new collection. The success of my first set of paintings was exhilarating, but this one feels special. The colours, the themes – they're all coming together perfectly. I can't wait to unveil it. I'm sure this one will be even bigger.

My first collection, themed around animals, had taken the art world by storm. Each piece was a vibrant exploration of form and movement, capturing the essence of wildlife in bold strokes and unexpected colours. There was the fierce grace of a lion mid-pounce, the delicate flutter of a hummingbird's wings, the stealthy elegance of a leopard creeping through the jungle. The pieces resonated with people, speaking to a primal connection between humanity and the animal kingdom. Critics praised the way I had brought a fresh perspective to a timeless subject, and the collection had sold out almost immediately.

But this new collection is different, more abstract. It delves into the concept of two worlds within one world. I've been exploring the idea of parallel realities, contrasting the mundane with the fantastical. One painting depicts a bustling cityscape, with shadowy figures moving through their daily routines, while above them, a dream like world of floating islands and ethereal creatures' hovers, almost within reach. Another piece shows a serene forest scene, but hidden within the trees are glimpses of an underwater realm, seething with vibrant marine life. The goal is to evoke a sense of wonder and possibility, to suggest that there is more to our world than meets the eye.

I can't wait to unveil it. The anticipation of seeing people's reactions, of watching them get lost in the layers and interpretations, fills me with excitement. This one feels special, like I'm on the cusp of something truly groundbreaking.

My thoughts are interrupted by the sound of Mike's voice, raised in frustration. He's in the study, as usual. I walk closer, curious and a bit concerned, and hear him talking on the phone.

"What? How many pages? Twenty-five! Happy?... I'll get you the book in time just stop calling me every five fucking minutes."

Mike hangs up abruptly. I hear the phone hit the wood of the table with force.

"Agent?" I ask, stepping into the doorway.

Mike turns to the sound of my voice, clearly agitated. "Yeah... The guy really gets on my nerves."

"When are you due to deliver to the publishers?" I ask, trying to sound supportive.

"Six weeks ago," he admits.

"That's not good. Are you even close?" I press gently.

"I'm at least 150 pages away from being done," he confesses, a note of despair in his voice.

I sigh softly. "I guess you're not coming to bed anytime soon then."

He looks at me without saying a word, but that's enough. I understand. I linger for a moment, contemplating how to approach what's really on my mind.

"Mike?" I ask quietly.

"Yeah?"

"Can I ask you something?" I venture, my voice hesitant.

"Sure," he replies, though I can hear the hesitation in his voice.

"Where did you go today?" I ask, trying to keep my tone light, but the question carries weight.

"Where did I go? Nowhere... I've been here writing," he says quickly.

"Are you sure?" I press, watching his reaction closely.

"Yeah, Rhea, what's with the fucking third degree? I just told you I'm way past my deadline. I don't have time to go anywhere," he snaps, irritation flaring.

I fall silent for a moment, weighing my next words.

"Do you mind? I have work to do," he adds, his tone softer but still strained.

I hesitate, then ask, "Why were your house keys stuck in the door?"

His eyes widen for a fraction of a second. He hadn't realized he'd left them there. "Oh that... I went down to buy a coke zero," he replies quickly.

I can tell he's scrambling. Something doesn't add up. "Instamart wasn't delivering because of some rider strike," he adds, trying to sound casual.

I nod slowly, deciding to let it go for now. "Okay... Night," I say, turning towards the bedroom.

"Night," he echoes.

I walk over to the bedroom, feeling a knot of unease settle in my stomach. Something isn't right. Mike seems so agitated and distant tonight, and it's unsettling. I was so excited to tell him about my day at the studio, about how well the new collection is coming along, but the look on his face and the edge in his voice made it impossible. Instead, I'm left with this growing sense of loneliness, even though he's right here in the house with me. It's like he's physically present but emotionally elsewhere. I miss not being able to talk to him, he's always been my biggest supporter. Right now, it feels like there's a wall between us, and I can't help but worry about what's on the other side.

XVII

MIKE

I couldn't sleep at all last night. My mind was stuck on that damn video of Natasha and me. It played on loop in my head, every detail searing itself into my brain. It's unimaginable how something so beautiful and poetic could turn into something so traumatic and scaring. How the hell did someone film us? My secret is going to come out, and everything is going to go to shit soon if I don't figure out a way to stop this. I need a plan, and I need it fast. I'm starting to regret ever sending that message. What happened in London should have stayed in London.

Rhea and I sit at the breakfast table, eating in silence. She's buried in a book while I pretend to watch the news on my iPad. The energy between us is different from our usual breakfasts. An awkward silence hovers around the room, thick and heavy. My mind drifts back to the previous night, wondering how I could have been so careless to leave my keys in the door. Rhea found them and now I'm sure she suspects that I'm up to something. The tension is palpable, making it hard to think straight.

The bell rings. Rhea puts her book down and is about to get up when I drop the iPad on the table and rush to door, yelling out to her as I do it.

"You sit, I'll get it. Must be that asshole kid again."

I rush to the door and open it. It's not an asshole kid but another asshole black envelope. Quickly picking it up, I look around. The lift is on my floor. I rush down the stairs, stumbling along the way.

I burst out of the building lobby and look around. Nothing out of the ordinary. My eyes go to the gate. No one there other than the security guard. I rush to the guard.

"Did you see anyone walk out of the building just now?"

"No, sir. No one left."

"Did anyone enter the building? In the last fifteen or twenty minutes?"

"No, sir. I've been right here."

Frustration bubbles up inside me. How the fuck do these envelopes keep landing at my door? I make my way back into the building and get into the elevator.

I come out of the lift on my floor. The door is still open. I shut the elevator door. As I turn around, I notice Rhea walking towards the door. My eyes go to ANOTHER envelope sitting on the doormat. I quickly jump forward and step on top of the envelope to hide it. Rhea arrives at the door at the same time and jumps back in fright as I jump in front of the door.

"What the fuck is wrong with you?" she exclaims.

"Sorry, sorry! I just got an idea for a scene that I've been stuck on for a few days."

"You're acting so weird."

I don't respond. Rhea walks back into the house. I quickly pocket the other envelope and take a quick look around. Still, no one there. I enter the house and shut the door.

Rhea is in the kitchen putting away the dishes and the left-over food. I sneak past and go into my study, shutting the door behind me.

I sit at my desk, heart pounding, and open the black envelopes. I need to know what's inside, what new nightmare I'm about to face. I slide the contents out, dreading what I'll find.

Inside the first envelope is a USB drive. My hands tremble as I plug it into my laptop. A video file pops up, and with a deep breath, I press play. The screen fills with the familiar, dreaded scene of Natasha and me in her bungalow. My heart sinks further. I yank out the flash drive and slip it into my pocket.

I open the second envelope, finding a single piece of paper. My stomach drops as I see the message, each letter cut out from a magazine like a ransom note. It reads: "More to come. Be ready." My mind races, trying to understand who could be doing this and why. The fear and paranoia grow stronger. How the fuck did they manage to get this footage? And what do they want from me?

My phone buzzes, pulling me out of my frantic thoughts. It's a message from my agent, saying the publishers have sent a strong email stating that I have to deliver a first draft in the next 7 days. When things go wrong, they have a way of cascading all at once, like a dam breaking under pressure, unleashing chaos in every direction.

A knock on the study door startles me. "Mike? Are you okay?" Rhea's voice is gentle, concerned, as she pops her head into the room.

"Yeah, I'm fine," I lie, quickly shutting the laptop and shoving the envelopes into a drawer. "Just working through a tough scene."

"Are you sure? You've been acting strange all morning."

"I'm fine," I insist, trying to sound reassuring. "Just under a lot of pressure with the deadline."

She lingers for a moment before sighing. "Alright. I'm heading to the studio. I'll see you in the evening."

"Okay, see you later," I say, forcing a smile. As she walks away, the weight of my secrets presses down even harder. I need to figure out who's behind this and how to stop them before everything falls apart.

XVIII
NATASHA

Loud music blares from the Bluetooth speaker, Katy Perry's "Roar" filling the room with energy. I'm running on the treadmill in my living room, drenched in sweat. I've been at it for a while, pushing myself harder and harder, trying to outrun the mess in my head. The situation with Mike has been consuming me – the secrecy, the constant fear of being found out, and the guilt that gnaws at me. I've been telling myself that running will help clear my mind, but all it does is amplify the chaos.

I hear the doorbell ring. I slow down the speed on the treadmill and then hop off. Grabbing the hand towel from the railing, I wipe the sweat off my face as I walk over to the door. On the other side is our Baillie Gifford Prize-winning author, Mr. Mikesh Kharbanda. He looks incredibly stressed, his expression tense and weary. He holds up two black envelopes in his hand. My stress levels escalate to match Mike's.

We move back inside the house, the tension palpable. I stand by the fridge, sipping water from my sipper. Mike sits on a stool next to the kitchen counter, both envelopes laid out in front of him. In the distance, from the other room, Katy Perry is still roaring.

"It really feels like this person's only agenda is for Rhea to find out," Mike says, frustration clear in his voice. "They're trying very hard to make sure she gets her hands on one of these envelopes. The notes inside, with letters cutout from magazines, almost feels professional or like someone who watches too many crime movies."

"It's creepy," I reply, shivering slightly despite the sweat still drying on my skin. "But whoever is doing this knows what they're doing. They're playing a twisted game."

I take one last sip of water before setting down the sipper on the table in front of me. Walking up to Mike, I try to think clearly, "Is there any way you can convince Rhea to take a trip or something?"

"What? Why would I do that?" he asks, bewildered.

"Mike, this person doesn't look like they're going to stop this anytime soon, and you're not going to always manage to open the door before her."

"But here I can still keep an eye on her and make sure that she doesn't get her hands on one. If she's somewhere else and this person finds out or follows her or something... I'm screwed.

I almost correct him, wanting to point out that I'm just as screwed as he is, but this isn't the time for that. Instead, I continue, "I know what you mean, but I still think it's safer to keep her out of the house, or out of the city if that's possible. With sending her away, there are a lot of ifs and buts that we can't be sure of, but if she's in the house, she's going to eventually get to one. Think about it."

Mike sighs heavily, rubbing his temples. "I'm too stressed to think clearly. My mind is a disastrous mess."

"You just need to take a load off," I suggest, sliding a few items from the countertop onto the floor and hopping up on the counter. "That's something that I can help with."

Mike gets up and walks over to me. "Natahsa, now is not the time for this. We need to get to the bottom of this, and fast. Your neck is on the line too, remember?"

I feel a pang of guilt but at the same time I'm glad that he's acknowledged my situation as well. "Sorry, you're right. We need to figure this out."

I hop down from the counter, trying to push aside the brief flicker of desire that had crossed my mind. Mike is right; we need to focus. The stakes are too high for distractions.

He looks away, his eyes distant, clearly needing time to process. "I need some space to figure out how to handle this. Maybe I'll talk to Rhea about going somewhere, just to keep her away from this mess before it's too late."

I place a hand on his arm, trying to convey all the reassurance I can muster. "Mike, I know this is overwhelming, but we will get through this. You're not alone in this. We'll figure it out together, I promise."

Mike nods, a flicker of hope in his eyes. "Alright, I'll talk to her. Maybe it's the best option."

As he agrees, a thought crosses my mind. If Rhea leaves town, it's good for us. With her out of the way, we can focus on finding out who's behind all of this rather than constantly worrying about keeping the information from her. It would give us the space and time we need to tackle this head-on.

Just as the tension begins to ease, the doorbell rings again. Mike and I exchange a wary glance. I walk over and open the door cautiously, finding yet another black envelope lying on the doorstep. My heart sinks as I pick it up and show it to Mike.

Without a word, Mike bolts out of the house, scanning the street frantically for any sign of the culprit. I watch from the doorway as he runs up and down the street, checking corners and alleys, but he returns empty-handed, frustration etched into his features.

"Did you see anyone?" I ask, as the fear kicks in.

"No," he says, breathless and defeated. "No one. It's like they're a ghost."

Mike takes the envelope from my hand, ripping it open with a mixture of dread and frustration. Inside is a note, the letters cut out from a magazine just like the previous ones, spelling out: "He's a married man."

Mike's face pales further. "This is getting out of control. They're relentless."

"Whoever it is, they're determined to ruin you, and now they're after me too" I say, feeling the gravity of the situation settle even more heavily.

"FUCK!" Mike explodes. "Why! Why! Why! This is so fucked up. We never should have got into this fucking mess!"

XIX
RHEA

Mike is standing by the door, trying to convince me to leave with him. He has a meeting with his agent, and he wants to drop me off at the studio on the way.

"Rhea, come on. We can go together. I'll drop you off and then head to my meeting, it's on the way," he insists, a hint of urgency in his voice.

I smile, trying to hide the uneasiness brewing inside me. "It's alright, Mike. I have a few things to take care of here first. You go ahead. I'll be fine."

"We can stop by The Bagel Shop and get you your favourite coffee and a salmon and cream cheese bagel?" he adds with a hopeful smile, knowing how much I love their fresh bagels and the rich aroma of their coffee.

"Mike! Just go please, you'll be late. I'll leave when I'm ready."

He looks at me for a moment, as if sensing that something is off. But he doesn't press further. "Alright, if, you're sure. I'll see you later then."

"I'll see you later," I echo, watching as he grabs his bag and leaves the house.

As soon as the door closes behind him, I feel a wave of relief wash over me. I need time to think, to figure out what's going on. My mind is a whirlwind of thoughts and suspicions. The awkwardness from yesterday is still looming in the air between us.

I call Nandini, my assistant. "Nandini, I'm running a little late. I have some stuff to take care of at home. I'll be at the studio in an hour."

Hanging up the phone, I stand outside Mike's study door, my heart pounding. I hesitate for a moment before turning the handle and stepping inside. The room smells faintly of coffee and weed, a familiar scent that usually brings me comfort. Today, it only heightens my anxiety.

Mike's laptop sits in the centre of his cluttered desk. I walk up to it, my hands trembling slightly as I open it. In the six years that we've been together, not once have I ever looked at any of his work without his permission but this time, I can't stop myself. The screen flickers to life, and I enter the password. I've always known his password, but I'm not sure if he's aware of that. I feel a pang of guilt for invading his privacy, but my curiosity and concern outweigh it.

The word file titled – "The Affair" is open on the screen, halfway through chapter 3. I scroll up to the top and begin to read. The words seem to leap off the screen, pulling me into a world that feels eerie and uncomfortable.

The first chapter describes a clandestine affair, filled with passion and deceit. The protagonist, a successful screenwriter, is entangled in a web of lies that threaten to unravel his entire life. My eyes widen as I read further. The description, the settings, the emotions – they are all too vivid, too real.

I know Mike's writing style well. He's known for his preachy self-help books that have made him a household name, but his attempts at fiction have always been lacklustre, rejected by publishers' time and again. This feels different. This feels too close to home. The fine line between fiction and reality blurs with each sentence I read, and a chill runs down my spine.

The protagonist's lover, a girl named Destiny, is described with striking accuracy. I can almost see the woman, with her athletic build and confident demeanour. The more I read, the more convinced I become that this in not just a work of fiction. This is Mike's secret life laid bare, disguised as a novel. The new found passion in Mike, from his trip to London, suddenly starts to make sense.

My heart races as I continue to read, my mind racing with questions. Is this what really happened in London? Is she the reason he missed the Baillie Gifford Prize ceremony? And who is this woman? The descriptions match no one I know in our social circle, but the fear of the unknown distresses me.

I lean back in the chair, closing my eyes for a moment. The room feels stifling, the walls closing in around me. The trust I have in Mike, the love we share – it all seems to crumble in the face of this new revelation. I read a few more pages and then shut the laptop. I can't read anymore. It's too much. I need to process what I have just read, to confront Mike and get the truth. I take a deep breath and walk out of the study, closing the door behind me.

As I make my way to the front door, my mind is a whirlwind of emotions. I feel a mix of anger, betrayal, and sadness. I love Mike, but the trust between us in now in question. I need answers, and I need them soon. I don't want my mind to wander until I hear it from him.

In the cab ride to the gallery, I replay the words I have read in my mind. The scenes, the emotions – they are too raw, too real. This book seems more like a confession than a made-up story.

At the gallery, I try to focus on my work, but my mind keeps drifting back to the book. I need to talk to Mike, to confront him about what I've read. But how can I do that without revealing that I have snooped through his things?

The day drags on, each minute feeling like an hour. I go through the motions, meeting with a few potential gallery owners about my new collection, but my heart isn't in it. I am consumed by the need to know the truth.

Finally, I decide to end the day early, I take a cab back home, my mind racing with what I will say to Mike. I need to be calm, to approach the situation with a clear head. But the emotions swirling inside me make that seem impossible.

As I walk through the front door, I hear the silence of the empty house. Mike hasn't returned yet. I check the time; he should have been back by now. A wave of anxiety washes over me. Is he with her? The thought makes my stomach churn. I want to call him, demand to know where his is, but I hesitate. What if I'm wrong? What if his meeting with his agent has just run longer than expected? They tend to do that sometimes.

I finally send him a message: When will you be back?

A few minutes later, my phone buzzes with his reply: Going with Ashish to meet the publishers. I'll be back late.

My heart sinks. I'm almost certain he's with the other woman, but I have to wait for him and get this all out in the open once and for all. I sit down on the couch, the house eerily quiet around me, and wait for Mike to come home, my mind filled with questions and doubts. Tonight, I need answers.

XX

NATASHA

I walk through the corridor of what seems to be a very fancy hotel, my heels clicking against the marble floor. The Incredible Hulk follows closely behind me, the one who's less green. His massive presence is a comforting shield. He's literally the closest thing to the Hulk that doesn't involve any CGI – towering, muscular, and imposing. We stop at the large double doors at the end of the hall, room 1001. Presumably the suite.

Dressed in a long black trench coat, I stand in the centre of the large living room area of the suite, the plush carpet soft beneath my heels. I take a moment to survey the room. Six men surround me, other than the Hulk, seated on the sofas placed around where I am standing. The stage is set for a performance. I turn to the Hulk, who presses play on a boombox that he's been lugging around all through. A song begins – "Pays to Know" by MYPET.

With a slow, deliberate motion, I let the trench coat slide off my body, revealing my 'fantasy outfit.' A checked red and black short skirt. White shirt knotted up just under the bustline. Sleazy old men with schoolgirl fantasies. How predictable! The Hulk hits a switch by the door and half the lights turn off. He usually does an extensive survey of the rooms prior to my performances to make sure there are no hidden cameras, so he always knows where everything is.

I start by swaying my hips to the rhythm, my movements fluid and tantalizing. The men's eyes are glued to me, their anticipation palpable. I run my hands slowly down my sides, feeling the fabric of my shirt tighten round my curves. My fingers play at the knot just under my bustline, teasingly tugging at it before letting go. I walk towards one of the men, my heels making impressions in the carpet, and lean in close enough that he can smell my perfume. I let my breath brush against his ear before pulling back and spinning away, leaving him wanting more.

As the beat picks up, I unbutton the first few buttons of my shirt, revealing a hint of lace underneath. I catch the eye of another man and give him a sultry wink. I turn around and face the Hulk, who stands firm, watching the men. I trail my fingers down to my legs, slowly lifting one to rest on the sofa, right between a man's legs. His breath hitches as I move in time with the music, unzipping my heeled boot with a deliberate slowness. I fling the boot behind me without looking, knowing the Hulk will catch it.

I perform a quick, sensual spin and plant my other foot between another set of legs. This time, I let my hand linger on the zipper, watching the man's reaction as I slowly undo it. The second boot joins the first in the Hulk's hands. Now barefoot, I feel more connected to the ground, more in control of the energy in the room.

The lights cast a soft glow on my skin as I untie the knot on my shirt, pulling it off in one smooth motion. I throw it across the room, and it lands on the face of one of the men. He pulls it down quickly, his eyes wide with excitement.

I am now in a lacy white bra that contrasts sharply with my red and black skirt. The room is filled with the scent of desire and the sound of their barely contained anticipation.

I move to the centre of the room, running my hands through my hair, letting it cascade over my shoulders. I slide my hands down my body, feeling every curve, every muscle, as if I am rediscovering myself. The skirt is the next to go. I unbutton it slowly, turning around to give the men a view of my back as I slide it down my legs. It pools at my feet, and I step out of it gracefully.

Now in just my lingerie, I approach one of the men, straddling his lap. I move sensuously, my hips gyrating to the beat of the music. His hands hover over, unsure of whether to touch. I lean in, my lips almost brushing his ear, and whisper, "Look, but don't touch. If you touch me, then he touches you," I say, gesturing towards the Hulk with my eyes. I feel the shiver that runs through him as I pull back, a wicked smile on my lips.

I move to the next man, repeating the tease, letting my hands glide over his chest, feeling his rapid heartbeat under my fingers. The men are entranced, their eyes following my every move, their breaths synchronized with my movements. The energy in the room is electric, a heady mix of power and desire.

I step back to the centre, running my hands over my body one last time, savouring the power I hold over them. The song builds to a dramatic climax, and I finish with a flourish, my body arching gracefully, my head thrown back in a final act of seduction.

The song comes to a dramatic end. I stand there in the bare minimum, my body glistening with a thin sheen of sweat. The sleaze applauds, their faces flushed with desire. They all get up and walk off into different parts of the suite, clearly needing some alone time after the performance. I am left standing, half naked, alone in the room. Well, the Hulk is there too, but he's sort of blended into the background by now.

The room is silent, except for the faint hum of the air conditioning. I walk over to the couch and pick up my clothes, the mask of seduction slipping away. This Natasha is starkly different from the one dancing just a few seconds ago. The performance is over, and the real me reemerges.

As I gather my discarded clothing, I feel the wright of their gazes still lingering on my skin, a reminder of the power I wield and the price I pay for it. Don't get me wrong, I love my job and I'm extremely good at it but this is my first time performing since I met Mike, and it just feels a bit different.

I glance at the Hulk, who gives me a small nod, his silent assurance grounding me. Despite the bravado and the seductive act, there's a bond between us – a mutual understanding of the roles we play in this twisted game.

I walk towards the door, my heart still racing from the adrenaline of the performance. Each step is a reminder of the duality I live with – Natasha, the seductress who commands attention and desire, and Natasha, the woman who longs for something real amidst the charade.

As I exit the suite, the corridor feels colder, the opulence of the hotel a stark contrast to the rawness of what just transpired. The mask is off, but the performance continues. As I stand, waiting for the elevator, my phone beeps. A message from Mike.

XXI

MIKE

The night is young, well, youngish. I drive into the building, turning right, and down into the path leading to the basement parking. I step out of the car, my mind a swirl of thoughts from my meeting with the publishers. Their threat to revoke the contract still lingers in my mind. The pressure is immense, and I know I need Rhea gone, but I have no idea how to broach the subject.

I open the door to the apartment, expecting to find Rhea in the living room, but she's not there. Instead, she's standing in the hallway, waiting for me. I lean in for a kiss, hoping to greet her with some semblance of normalcy, but she walks past me and enters the bedroom, leaving me hanging. I'm confused, and a knot of anxiety forms in my stomach. I need to smooth this over if I'm going to ask her to leave the house for a few days.

I take a breath, compose myself, and follow her into the bedroom. As I enter, I see her stuffing clothes into a half-packed suitcase lying on the bed. I'm taken aback. This is exactly what I wanted, but I haven't even said anything yet.

"What are you doing?" I ask, trying to keep my voice steady.

"Going to my mom's house," she replies curtly, not looking at me.

I want to ask why. What has suddenly made her want to leave? Did she get her hands on one of those black envelopes? But there's another thought that comes more spontaneously. "But... you hate going to your mom's house!"

Rhea stops what she's doing for a second and glares at me. That's not the reaction she was looking for. I mentally kick myself. "What I meant to say was... why are you going? What has happened?"

"Nothing. I just feel like it," she says, her tone dismissive.

"Rhea? Please," I implore. "Why are you doing this to me?"

"You're such a narcissist. Everything has to be about you, doesn't it?" she snaps, throwing more clothes into the bag.

"Okay, fine. If it's not about me, then what's it about?" I ask, trying to fight back.

Rhea's eyes flash with anger. "What it's about, Mike, is that I need space. I need to get away from here."

"But why now?" I press, feeling the frustration build inside me. "What's changed all of a sudden?"

Rhea pauses, her hands frozen mid-air, gripping a dress. She looks at me, her eyes narrowing. "You really don't get it, do you?"

"No, I don't," I admit, my voice rising. "Why don't you just tell me instead of packing up and running off?"

"Because it's always the same with you," she shoots back. "You never listen, you never see what's right in front of you."

"What am I supposed to see, Rhea?" I ask, exasperated. "That you're upset? That you're leaving without explaining why?" I'm not quite sure why I'm fighting so hard for something that I actually want, but I need to know what made her come to this decision.

"I'm leaving because I need to think," she says, her voice trembling with emotion. "And I can't do that here, not with you around."

I feel a pang of guilt. "Look, I'm sorry if I've been distant. I've got a lot on my plate with the book and the publishers breathing down my neck. They've threated to revoke my contract if I don't deliver a draft in the next three days."

"Is that all it is, Mike? Just the book?" she asks, her eyes searching mine.

"What else would it be?" I ask, feeling a knot of anxiety tighten in my chest.

Rhea sighs, shaking her head. "I don't know, Mike. You tell me."

She resumes packing, and I feel a surge of desperation. "Rhea, please. Don't go. Let's talk about this." I need her to believe that I want her to stay.

"Talk about what, Mike?" she asks, turning to face me. "About how you've been writing some fantasy about a woman named Destiny? About how it feels more real than anything you've ever written?"

My heart skips a beat. "Did you read my book?"

Rhea doesn't need to say anything. It's written all over her face. She might as well have YES printed on her forehead.

"First of all, no one names their kid 'Destiny' unless they want them to grow up and be a fucking stripper," she says, throwing a shoe across the room right at me. I manage to dodge it, barely.

"What the fuck, Rhea! First, you read my book without asking me, and then you have a fit about some made-up story? How childish can you be?" I shout, my frustration boiling over.

"Childish? Fuck you! I've read everything you've written in the last twelve years. You write preachy, self-help, pretentious, only-work-in-theory kind of crap. You can't write fiction if your life depended on it. This shit! What you've written... that's real! I can tell," she fires back, her words hitting harder than the shoe.

"So, you're going to storm out of her because I'm a great writer?" I ask, trying to deflect.

Rhea wants to throw the other shoe at me, but she stops herself. She shuts the suitcase. "Send me a copy when it's done and then we can talk differences between fact and fiction."

She walks out, leaving me standing alone in the apartment.

I slump down on the couch, a mix of emotions swirling inside me. I got what I wanted – Rhea has left – but not like this. She's read the book and is convinced that I'm having an affair, but she can't prove it. I'm not sure if this is a good thing or not. She was bound to find out eventually, but if she files for divorce on the grounds of adultery, I could lose everything. Under no circumstances can she get her hands on that video.

The truth is, I'm broke. Something that Rhea is completely unaware of. I poured most of my savings, from my parent's insurance policy, into buying out Rhea's first collection, hoping it would bolster her confidence and success. The remainder went to paying off critics for favourable reviews. All my earning from my book have gone into the house, maintaining our lavish lifestyle, and funding Rhea's inspirational retreats. I've basically given her all of my money to make her feel like she's earned it. The things we do for love. Now, I'm trapped in this mess.

On the grounds of adultery, she could get half of everything I have left. Even though half of nothing is still nothing, my reputation would be tarnished, and my career would crumble to dust.

I need to talk to someone. Natasha.

Later, I sit in the living room, a glass of whiskey in one hand and a joint in the other. A modern-day Devdas, if you can call it that. I pick up my phone from the table in front of me and start typing: *She's gone.* An immediate reply: *Where?*

Her mom's. Goa. Far enough. I send another message immediately after: *Come over? Need to talk.*

I wait for Natasha's response, my heart pounding. She replies: *Tomorrow? Please?*

I lock my phone screen, without replying, and put it down on the table. I knock back the remainder of the whiskey in the glass, take a big puff from the joint, and make my way to the study. The drama in my life is relentless. It's chaos, but it's also potential material for my book. You can't make this stuff up. Every argument, every secret, every hidden emotion – fodder for the pages that might save my career. The line between my fiction and reality is blurrier than ever, but perhaps that's where the magic lies. And so, like every other writer, I too, shall write through the pain.

XXII
RHEA

I stand in the lobby of our building, waiting for my Uber to arrive. The polished marble floors and sleek modern décor of the entrance feel cold and unwelcoming. The guard at the lobby reception gives me a sympathetic nod, sensing my distress but wisely keeping his distance. My mind is a whirlwind, a chaotic blend of emotions and thoughts.

Life, my choices, my future – all of it seems uncertain now. I replay the fight with Mike in my head, the hurtful words, the anger, the accusations. How did we get here? When did things start to fall apart? We used to be so happy, so in sync with each other. Now it feels like we're living in two different worlds. We never had secrets, but now, I'm not so sure.

I can't stop thinking about who this other woman might be. Mike never really admitted to having an affair, but his book, this damn book, it felt too real to be fiction. I think of the female character, Destiny, and the vivid, raw details Mike used to describe her. Who is she? Someone from his past? A figment of his imagination? Or someone very real, very present in his life right now?

Doubt creeps in, gnawing at the edges of my resolve. What if I'm wrong? What if I've made a terrible mistake? Mike's words echo in my mind, accusing me of being childish, of overreacting. But no, I can't let myself be swayed. I know what I read. I know how it made me feel. The truth is there, buried in his words, in the way he writes about this woman with such intensity.

I stand firm on my hunch. I have to. If I start doubting myself now, I'll never find the strength to move forward. The only way I'll change my stand on this is if he can convince me that this woman doesn't exist. The cab pulls up outside, and the guard steps out to open the door for me. I thank him with a small nod, my mind still racing.

As I slide into the back seat of the cab, the driver gives me a polite smile. I try to return it, but it feels forced, hollow. The driver pulls away from the lobby, and I stare back at the place that I call home, but it all feels different now.

We approach the gate of the building, and I see the other security guard standing there. He steps forward and signals the driver to stop. The cab comes to a halt, and the guard walks up to my window, holding a black envelope in his hand.

"Ma'am," he says, leaning in slightly. "Someone left this for you in the security cabin."

My heart skips a beat as I take the envelope from him. My name is print on the top of it in white ink. It feels ominous and out of place, a strange object intruding on my already tumultuous day. My hands tremble as I tear it open, my breath coming in shallow gasps.

"Who left this?" I ask the guard, my voice shaky.

He looks apologetic. "I don't know, ma'am. When I came back from the bathroom, it was lying on top of the entry register. I didn't see who left it."

Inside the envelope, there's a single piece of paper. The letters are cut out from magazines, forming a message. My eyes scan the words, my mind struggling to process what I'm reading. The cab driver watches me through the rearview mirror, concern etched on his face.

The message is clear, sending a chill down my spine. I sit back, my heart pounding in my chest. The envelope slips from my grasp, falling to the floor of the cab. I know that nothing will ever be the same again.

XXIII
NATASHA

The morning light filters through the curtains, casting a soft glow on the room. The air is thick with tension and desire. Mike's hands are on me, urgent and demanding, as if trying to escape the chaos of our lives through the intensity of our connection. His lips trail down my neck, leaving a path of fire in their wake. I arch my back, pressing closer to him, feeling the heat between us build to an almost unbearable level.

Our bodies move together, a dance of desperation and need. His touch is rough, almost frantic, as if he's trying to hold onto something slipping away. My fingers dig into his back, pulling him closer, wanting to lose myself in him. Every kiss, every caress, feels like both a plea and a promise, a way to forget everything outside this room.

Mike's breath is hot against my skin, mingling with my own gasps and moans. We move in perfect rhythm, each thrust bringing us closer to the edge. The intensity is overwhelming, a mix of passion and raw emotion that leaves us both trembling. There's an edge to our lovemaking, a sense of something unresolved lingering, just beneath the surface, driving us to push harder, to cling to each other as if our lives depend on it.

As the climax builds, our movements become more frantic, more desperate. The world outside fades away, leaving only the two of us, locked in this primal dance. And then, with a final, shuddering breath, we fall over the edge together, the release a cathartic burst of energy that leaves us both breathless and spent.

We collapse onto the bed, our bodies slick with sweat, hearts pounding in unison. The silence that follows is heavy, charged with the aftermath of our intense encounter. Mike lights a joint, the smoke curling up towards the ceiling. I slip into his shirt, the familiar fabric providing a small comfort.

"Is everything okay?" I ask, breaking the silence.

Mike gives a bitter chuckle. "Strange choice of question considering the situation."

"You know what I mean. Talk to me. Tell me what's going on in your head?"

He exhales a long plume of smoke. "Honestly, I feel badly about how I left things with Rhea. And then, there's this person. I need to know who the fuck is doing this. It's driving me insane."

"Look, as far as Rhea is concerned, just give her time to cool down a bit and then you guys can hash it out. And about this person... Is there anyone you can think of who might want to get back at you? An ex-girlfriend? An ex of hers maybe? You must have pissed off someone in all this time."

Mike shakes his head. "Strangely, no I haven't. Except that big guy from the restaurant in London. But he got his revenge."

He smirks, a glimmer of dark humour in his eyes. "Or maybe it's that Danny DeVito look-alike from the flight."

I laugh, but then pause, considering. "You know, he really looked like he wanted to kill you when we came out of the bathroom on the flight."

Mike turns to me, eyebrows raised. "What?"

"I wouldn't put it past him."

"No! Fuck no! What did I ever do to him?" he exclaims.

"You did me," I reply pointedly.

"And because if I hadn't, he would have had a shot?"

"Don't be an ass, Mike." I pause, trying to piece together this puzzle. "People have killed their own family for love, even lust... What's a stranger on a plane?"

Mike rolls his eye at my theory.

"You know what, fuck it! You go! Who do you think it could be?"

Mike is silent, clearly struggling to come up with anyone. But I can see the gears turning in his mind. He may have mocked my theory, but something about it is stuck in his head. Mike's eyes are fixed on the window in the bedroom, lost in thought.

"Let's say, for a second, hypothetically, that your theory holds water. What's next? How do we confirm this theory?" Mike asks, looking at me mockingly.

"We find him and we talk to him," I suggest.

"Oh, it's just that easy? For all we know he lives in London, or some other part of the world," Mike replies sceptically.

I pick up my phone and start dialling. Mike looks confused. "Who are you calling?" he asks.

I press the phone to my ear and wait. Cheesy hold music plays through the speaker. Mike looks at me, puzzled. I give him a reassuring nod.

"Hi, Karan... I like the name Karan, my ex-boyfriend's name was Karan," I say, trying to flirt my way through this.

Mike rolls his eyes at my lame attempt. But I push on, "I was on flight VA234 to Heathrow on April 6th at 1900 hours and there was a passenger seated in seat 1B. He left something valuable on the flight and I've been struggling to track him down for a while. No one has been able to help me. Hopefully you can, Karan?"

There is a theory in communication and psychology that suggests repeating someone's name in a conversation can help create a sense of intimacy and connection, which can be a subtle way to flirt. This technique can make the person feel special and noticed, as using their name can capture their attention and signal that you are genuinely interested in them. I'm trying to put this theory to the test.

"Of course I'll hold, Karan. You take your time." I pace around the room, trying to hide my impatience.

Karan comes back on the line. "Hi Karan... No, I absolutely understand you can't give out personal information just like that. If this was a call on your personal number, I'm sure you would have been able to do something. Unfortunately, I don't have your personal number, Karan."

Mike makes a fake gagging motion, but I ignore him. "Okay Karan, I understand. Thank you. You have a nice day too."

I hang up and look at Mike, "So? Shall we call Mr. DeVito with the number that Karan gave you?" he asks, smirking.

"The call was being recorded for training and quality purposes," I say with a smirk.

"So much for your plan," Mike mutters.

And at that exact moment, as though it were written in a script, my phone beeps. A message from an unknown number. It reads: *Hi Natasha ma'am :).* This is followed by the passenger's name, number, and address. I hold up the phone to show Mike. Karan signs off the message saying: *Now you have my personal number :)*

Mike's jaw drops. "Okay, so now what?"

"Now, you play with yourself while I flirt my way into round two," I say, winking at him as I head into the living room, shutting the bedroom door behind me.

I lean against the closed door for a moment, taking a deep breath. The tension is palpable. The stakes are high, and the sense of urgency is overwhelming. I need to get a meeting with this man. I make the call. The moment of truth.

XXIV

MIKE

I stand in the elevator, AirPods in my ears, waiting patiently to arrive at my floor. The song of the moment – "The Devil Inside" by Daniel Murphy, Anthony Sanudo, and Eric Serna. The elevator stops, and I step out, the music continuing to play as I make my way to my apartment.

I plonk myself on the couch and open my little box. Half a joint waits inside. I spark it up, needing the release it promises. I look at my phone screen, the contacts page open to Rhea's name. I want to make the call, but hesitation roots me in place.

The guilt gnaws at me, even as I inhale deeply from the joint. The smoke does little to calm my nerves. Finally, I decide to call her. The phone rings, each second dragging on painfully. No answer.

I sigh, my attempt to mend things with Rhea falling flat. I place the phone on the table, resigned. The tension is unbearable, and I need to focus on something that I can control. I head to my study, determined to pour my restless energy into writing.

I lean back in my study chair, the glow of my laptop screen illuminating the dark room. I decide to channel my frustration into writing, the one aspect of my life where I can direct the narrative. With less than forty-eight hours to the deadline, I need to get this thing done before another part of my life falls apart. I open the document for my novel, tentatively titled – 'The Affair', now morphing from a simple piece of fiction erotica into something far more complex and dark.

I begin typing, my fingers flying over the keys as scenes unfold in my mind. The protagonist, a tormented screenwriter named Kabir, finds himself entangled in a web of deceit and danger. His affair with a seductive dancer named Destiny, who performs in a seedy underground club, is just the beginning. The illicit thrill quickly turns into a nightmare when Kabir starts receiving threatening messages, each more ominous that the last.

Destiny's performances are vividly detailed, each one a blend of sensuality and danger. She dances with a ferocity that captivates and terrifies, her eyes locking onto Kabir's with an intensity that promises both pleasure and peril. The club's dark atmosphere, filled with shadows and whispers, heightens the tension. Kabir watches, entranced, as Destiny removes her clothing piece by piece, her movements both a seduction and a warning.

In the next scene, Kabir receives a black envelope, much like the ones I've been finding. Inside, a note composed of cut-out magazine letters reads: "Your secret is out.: The chilling message sends Kabir into a spiral of paranoia. He suspects everyone around him, from his aloof wife to his mysterious neighbour. The boundary between his reality and his writing blurs, each word he types drawing him deeper into a world where trust is a rare commodity and danger lurks in every shadow.

I write about Kabir's increasing desperation, his need to uncover who is behind the threats. His encounters with Destiny become more intense, their lovemaking tinged with a sense of impending doom. She becomes both his muse and his tormentor, her allure pulling him further into the darkness. The more he tries to extract himself from the situation, the deeper he gets entangled.

Kabir's mood becomes a battlefield, every thought a clash between his fear and his desire. He starts to see Destiny everywhere, her image haunting him even when she's not around. The scenes grow more frenzied, more disjointed, mirroring Kabir's unravelling psyche. The narrative takes on a life of its own, each twist and turn reflecting my own spiralling thoughts.

Just as I'm getting into the flow, my phone beeps. Natasha's message: "We've got him." I blink, momentarily disoriented, as the lines between my fiction and reality blur. Relief washes over me, but it's tinged with the ever-present anxiety that has become a part of my daily existence.

Driving to Natasha's house, my mind races. What's the play now that we've tracked down Mr. DeVito? Natasha seems convinced that he's our guy but I'm still not convinced.

Natasha is sitting on the edge of the bed, dressed in the same black trench coat I've seen her wear before. I pace up and down the room, anxiety troubling me. Natasha stands and walks over, taking my hands in hers.

"Don't worry. I've got this. We're very close to the truth," she says, her voice steady.

"I don't think you should be going alone. The man could be dangerous. If he's actually the person whose been sending the notes, all bets are off. He could do something to you. It's not safe, Natasha." I protest, my worry evident.

Natasha smiles, a mix of reassurance and determination in her eyes. "I've dealt with sleazy men most of my adult life. Besides, I have the Hulk. He'll be waiting right outside the whole time, just in case something goes wrong."

"Maybe I should go with you, we can talk to him together and get to the bottom of this." I say, hoping she will take me along.

"No, Mike... If he's our guy, he's not going to say a word in front of you. He's clearly after you, not me. I can get him to talk. Just trust me, please. I'll be fine," she says, sounding confident.

"Okay. Please be careful," I plead, feeling a knot of dread tightening in my stomach. "And don't do anything that I wouldn't do," I say, trying to lighten the mood.

She kisses me on the cheek and leaves, her trench coat sweeping behind her. I watch her go, a mix of admiration and fear battling within me.

I sit on the bed, looking out the open window, as Natasha's car drives off. The stress is palpable. I pick up my phone, staring at the screen for a few seconds before sending a message to Rhea: "Please call, I need to talk to you." The dual concern for both women weighs heavily on me.

I pace up and down the room, trying to stay focused. I keep checking my watch, the minutes ticking by agonizingly slowly. I light up a joint, hoping to calm my nerves. Both women are out of my reach, and the only solace I have is knowing – or at least believing – that I know where they are. But I can't shake the feeling that something is about to go terribly wrong.

XXV

NATASHA

The night is heavy with tension as I pull into the driveway. I see Mike pacing outside the house, a bundle of nervous energy. His eyes snap to mine as I step out of the car, searching for answers. I can feel the weight of his worry pressing down on both of us. He walks over to me and embraces me.

"I'm so glad you're okay," he says, pulling away. "What happened? Is it him? Mike demands, his voice tight with urgency.

"It is," I confirm, watching as his expression darkens.

"I'm going to kill that motherfucker," he growls, fists clenching at his sides.

"Calm down, Mike," I say, guiding him inside and closing the door behind us. "There's no need for that. You'll just get into even more trouble. I took care of it."

"What did you do?" His eyes bore into mine, a mix of fear and curiosity.

"Let's just say that he's not going to come near either of us again."

"Let's please say more, Natasha. What did you do? I want to know everything."

Taking a deep breath, I begin to recount the evening's events.

I parked the car in the driveway of a fancy bungalow. The lights from the house cast an eerie glow on the perfectly manicured lawn. "If I'm not back in 30 minutes, come get me," I said to The Hulk, my voice steady despite the butterflies in my stomach. I stepped out of the car, revealing my outfit that was hidden under my trench coat – a slutty version of an elf costume, complete with thigh-high red and white socks. I took a deep breath and walked up to the door.

Inside, Mr. DeVito, who we now know as Mr. Verma, dressed in a Santa costume, greeted me with a lecherous grin. His eyes widened in delight as he saw me dangling a pair of handcuffs. I smiled seductively, leading him to a chair where I secured his hands behind his back. With a flick of my wrist, I pressed play on the boombox I'd brought along, and a sultry version of "Jingle Bells" filled the room.

I danced around him, my movements slow and deliberate. His eyes followed me, lust and confusion battling for dominance on his face. I straddled his lap, running my hands over his chest, down to his stomach, and finally to his crotch. I squeezed his 'Jingle bells' tightly in the palm of my hand. He was panting, a mix of excitement and fear.

With one swift move, I removed my sock and stuffed it into his mouth, muffling his groans. "Jingle bells, motherfucker," I whispered in his ear, my voice dripping with venom. His eyes widened in realization as the fun drained from his face.

"Why are you sending those flash drives?" I demanded, tightening my grip on his crotch.

He mumbled something incoherent. I pulled the sock out of his mouth. "What flash drives?" he gasped, his voice high-pitched and strained.

"If you keep lying to me, I'll stop playing nice," I warned, squeezing harder. He whimpered, his resolve crumbling.

"I swear I didn't do anything!" he cried, tears welling in his eyes.

"Tell me the truth, or I'll make sure you never forget this night," I hissed.

"That asshole was cheating on his wife," he blurted out. "He doesn't deserve a woman like you. I did all this to protect you."

I leaned in close, my lips brushing his ear. "I'm a big girl, I can take care of myself. I don't need to be protected. Do not fuck with us. I'm only going to say this once. Whatever is happening between Mike and I is between the two of us, it has nothing to do with you. If you come anywhere near Mike or me again..." I let the threat hang in the air, releasing my grip on him. He gasped for breath, his face a mask of pain and humiliation.

Stepping back, I delivered a final blow, kicking him in the chest and sending the chair crashing to the ground. He lay there, helpless and defeated. I gathered my things and left the house, leaving the keys to the handcuffs by the door, his pitiful cries echoing behind me.

Back in the present, I watch as Mike processes my story. His face is a mix of relief and horror.

"Are you sure he won't come after us again? he asks, his voice barely above a whisper.

"I'm sure," I say, squeezing his hand reassuringly. "We're safe now."

Mike takes a deep breath, the tension slowly leaving his body. "Thank you," he murmurs, pulling me into a tight embrace.

As we stand there, holding each other, I can't help but feel a lingering unease. We may have dealt with DeVito, but the shadows of our actions will follow us. For now, though, we can breathe a little easier. We've survived another day.

Mike sits on the bed, and I sit next to him. His face is all tense, eyes filled with a mixture of disbelief and anger.

"I can't believe it was that fat motherfucker all along. What a fucking creep," he says, shaking his head. "Did you really need to put on a show for him though? Couldn't you have just got straight to the point?"

"Does that make you jealous?" I ask, a playful smile tugging at my lips.

Mike doesn't say anything, but the look on his face says it all. I gently push him flat out onto the bed and get on top of him.

"You poor baby. Let me make it up to you," I whisper, leaning in to kiss him. He barely reacts.

"What's wrong? Aren't you relieved?"

"I haven't been able to reach Rhea all day. I'm worried," he admits.

"Mike!" I cup his face in my hands, making him look at me. "We got him. Soon this will all be behind us, and I'm sure you and Rhea will work things out. When that happens, this, what we have, it's going to be on hold, indefinitely. But right now, let's make the most of the time we have before you catch your flight back to reality."

Mike takes a moment, his eyes searching mine. "When you put it like that..."

I take out my phone and quickly hit a few buttons. A song starts playing loudly, filling the room with Zayn's "Pillow talk." I take off the trench coat and toss it across the room to reveal my elf costume.

"Merry Christman to me," Mike mutters, his voice tinged with a hint of acceptance as I move closer to him.

The room pulses with the sultry beats of the song, each note weaving a tapestry of desire and intimacy around us. The music creates a rhythm that matches our movements, setting the stage for the intensity that follows.

Mike switches positions with me, his hands sliding gently but firmly along my sides as he moves on top. His eyes, dark with lust and something deeper, hold mine captive. He leans in, his lips capturing mine in a kiss that is both tender and demanding. His tongue teases my mouth open, deepening the kiss, making my heart race.

He slowly trails kisses down my neck, each one sending shivers of anticipation through my body. As his mouth moves lower, he pauses at the curve of my breasts, taking a moment to savour the softness of my skin. His hand caress me, fingers tracing delicate patterns that ignite fires wherever they touch. I moan softly, my hands tangling in his hair, urging him on.

Mike's kisses continue their journey, exploring my stomach, his breath hot against my skin. He looks up at me, a mischievous smile playing on his lips, before he lowers his head further. The sensation of his mouth on me makes me gasp, my back arching off the bed. I can't help but push my head deeper into the pillow, the pleasure overwhelming.

A loud moan escapes my lips, echoing through the room, blending with the music. Mike moves back up, his face flushed, eyes sparkling with satisfaction and desire. He looks at me, our breaths mingling, the connection between us electric.

"My turn," I whisper, voice thick with need. I flip him over, straddling him. Our bodies fit together perfectly, like pieces of a puzzle. I lean down, kissing him deeply, tasting the remnants of my pleasure on his lips. Slowly, I begin to slide down his body, trailing kisses along his chest, feeling his muscles tense under my touch. His skin is warm, the scent of him intoxicating.

As I reach his hips, I can feel his anticipation, his need mirroring my own. I tease him, my hands and mouth exploring, eliciting groans of pleasure that resonate through him. His head is thrown back, eyes closed, lost in sensation.

We switch again, our bodies moving in a dance as old as time. Mike is back on top, his hands firm and confident as he positions himself. The foreplay has stoked the flames of our desire, and now, it's time for the final connection. He enters me slowly, the sensation making us both gasp. We move together, finding a rhythm that builds and builds, each thrust bringing us closer to the edge.

Mike's eyes never leave mine, his gaze intense and filled with emotions I can't quite decipher. His hands roam my body, caressing, teasing, making me feel worshipped. The pleasure is almost too much, my body trembling beneath him as we movie in perfect sync.

Our moans become louder, more desperate. The sensation is overwhelming, the connection deepening with every movement. I cling to him, nails digging into his back, needing to anchor myself to something solid as the pleasure builds to an unbearable peak.

With a sudden move, Mike shifts us into a different position. He kneels, pulling me onto his lap. I wrap my legs around his waist, our bodies pressed tightly together. He thrusts upward, his hands gripping my hips to guide me. The new angle sends waves of pleasure coursing through me, making me cry out.

"God, Mike," I moan, my hands clutching his shoulders as I move in sync with him. He responds with a guttural groan, his lips finding mine in a hungry kiss. The kiss is raw and rough, mirroring the intensity of our movements.

He pulls back, flipping me over onto my hands and knees. I feel his hands on my hips, steadying me as he enters me from behind. The sensation is deeper, more intense. I can't help but cry out as he sets a relentless pace. His hands travel up my spine, sending shivers through me, before locking into my hair to pull me back against him with each thrust.

"Natahsa," he growls, his voice thick with lust. "You feel incredible."

"Yes, Mike, just like that," I gasp, pushing back against him, matching his rhythm. The room fills with the sounds of our bodies colliding, our moans and gasps creating a symphony of raw passion.

He pulls out suddenly, and I whimper at the loss. Before I can protest, he flips me onto my back again. He enters me swiftly, our bodies fitting together perfectly. His thrusts are urgent, powerful, driving us both towards the edge. His hand slides between us, finding that sensitive spot, his fingers working in tandem with his thrust.

"Oh God, Mike," I cry, my back arching off the bed. "I'm so close."

"Me too," he pants, his pace quickening. "Come with me, Natasha."

The intensity is almost too much to bear. I feel the pressure building, the pleasure overwhelming. With one final, deep thrust, we both cry out, the world dissolving into a blinding haze of ecstasy. The release is explosive, waves of pleasure crashing over us, leaving us both trembling and breathless.

Mike collapses beside me, pulling me close. His lips brush against mine in a tender kiss, his breath warm and soothing.

"I think I might be falling in love with you," he whispers, his voice raw with emotion.

I am speechless, the weight of the words sinking in. this was supposed to be an affair, a distraction. But now, it feels like so much more. I kiss him back, unable to find the words to express the whirlwind of emotions inside me. I smile, letting him see the warmth, the affection, and the confusion all mixed together in my eyes.

As we lay there, the afterglow of our lovemaking surrounding us, I can't help but wonder what the future holds. The present is a tangled mess of pleasure and pain, of secrets and truths. For now, all I can do is hold onto this moment, this connection with Mike, and hope that somehow, we will find a way to navigate the storm together.

XXVI

MIKE

I'm standing by the bed, struggling to pull on my t-shirt. My pants are already on, but my mind is still with Natasha, who's lying under the covers, sipping on a glass of water. Hydration is important, especially after what we just did.

"Are you sure you don't want to stay back? We could indulge in boundary-pushing activities," Natasha teases, her eyes glinting with mischief.

"Would that I could. It's just... this whole thing is still a mess in my head. Rhea won't even speak to me and here I seem to be falling in love with you," I admit, my voice tinged with frustration.

"Quite a pickle," she responds, with a knowing smile.

"That's one way of looking at it. I just need to go home and be a hundred percent sure there are no more envelopes. That will make me feel a little better. Then I can sort this whole Rhea situation out and then maybe... Maybe, we could talk about us?" I say, trying to find a way through the chaos.

Natasha smiles and walks up to me. She kisses me on the cheek. "Maybe."

She walks me to the door, now dressed in her robe, and kisses my goodbye. "I know right now it seems like everything is falling apart but soon this will all be over and life will get back on track. I promise."

"I know it will. Everything falls apart at some point," I say, glancing past her to the wall at the end of the corridor. "Even the Mona Lisa is falling apart."

Natasha turns and notices the Mona Lisa, that's hung on her wall, is slightly tilted. She looks at me with a smile. One last kiss before I leave.

As I turn on the lights of my car and drive out of the driveway, I catch a final glimpse of Natasha, stationed at the door, watching me leave. She shuts the door as I exit the premises.

Driving through the dimly lit streets of Bandra, my mind is a whirlwind of conflicting thoughts and emotions. The steering wheel feels like the only solid thing in my life right now, grounding me in this moment of transition between two worlds.

I was with Natasha as an escape from my reality, a brief respite from the chaos that has become my life. But now, that escape is turning into a reality of its own, drawing me in with a force I hadn't anticipated. The walls around my life are closing in slowly and I have to get out before it's too late.

I need to find a way to end things with Rhea, without her finding out about Natasha. The thought of losing everything in the divorce – my home, my career, my dignity – is too much to bear. If Rhea finds out about Natasha, the fallout with be catastrophic. But if I can navigate this delicate situation, if I can manage to end things amicably, then maybe I can explore this new chapter with Natasha. There are some truths about her that need to be uncovered too but it would make a great next chapter in my life as well as a perfect ending for my book.

My book. The irony isn't lost on me. The fiction I'm writing is starting to mirror my reality in ways I hadn't intended when I first started out. The character, the situations – they're all reflections of my tangled emotions and the mess I've made of my personal life.

And then there's the matter of something Natasha has kept from me. Something significant that I know but she doesn't know that I know. I need to confront her about it before anything moves forward, but not tonight. One crisis at a time.

The streetlights blur as I drive through the city, my mind racing ahead to the conversation I need to have with Rhea. I need to speak with her as soon as possible. I need to be honest, but not too honest. I need to end things, but not in a way that will ruin me. It's a tightrope walk, and the stakes couldn't be higher. One wrong move, one slip, and everything could come crashing down.

The road ahead seems to stretch endlessly as I reach for my phone. I dial a number. Calling "The Law." Mom-in-law. The voice on the other end is familiar and sharp.

"Did the sun come up in the west?

"Hey."

"Hey? Wow! No snarky comeback... Is everything okay, Mike?"

"Working on it. Could I please speak to Rhea? Just for a minute?"

"Rhea?" she asks, confusion in her tone.

"Yeah... I've been trying to call her all day but she's not answering my calls, so I thought I'd see if you'd help me out."

"But why are you calling me to talk to Rhea? I'm confused."

"She's staying with you, that's why?"

"What? What are you talking about? I haven't spoken to her in over a week."

"What the fuck! Sorry. She left yesterday, to come to you. She's not at home."

"Why was she coming to me? And why didn't anyone tell me?" she says, her voice sounding genuine.

"We had a moment of friction and she thought it's best to stay away for a couple of days. I thought she would have talked to you."

"Well, she hasn't. And besides, if she wanted a break from you, coming to me isn't the best idea. That's like leaving one stressful environment only to jump into another. You know what our relationship is like, don't you, Mike?"

Rhea's relationship with her mother has always been distant, strained by years of unresolved tensions and unspoken words. I had been surprised when she said she wanted to go to her mom's, but given how upset she was that day, I didn't read too much into it at the time.

"But then where did she go?" I ask, the gears turning in my brain.

"You think she'd tell me? She's a big girl, Mike. She'll be fine. Maybe she went to a hotel or to stay with a friend."

Something doesn't make sense, but I don't have much to go on. "Could you call her? Just let me know if she's fine?"

"Yeah, I can try. I'll let you know once I speak with her."

I hang up and continue to drive. A distressing worry settles in my chest. Maybe Rhea has gone to a hotel to get some alone time, or maybe to see a friend, but what if she hasn't? I'm trying to figure out my next move. If there even is one.

I'm closer to home now, the familiar streets bringing no comfort. A message notification sound breaks the silence. I check the message on the car screen. It's from "The Law." *'Phone is off. Tried three times.'* My concern deepens.

I pull over to the side of the road, reaching behind my seat for my bag. I pull out my laptop and open it, logging into Google Maps. Given the situation, I believe that a little violation of Rhea's privacy would be forgiven. I log into her account and check the last location of her phone. The perks of being in a trusted relationship – knowing your partner's passwords. I see the last registered location from an hour ago.

My heart pounds as I zoom in on the map. I feel a chill run down my spine. "What the fuck," I whisper to myself, my mind racing with possibilities. I start the car and turn the car around, heading towards the unknown, hoping to find answers and fearing what I might discover. I call my agent on the way. If there's anyone who knows how to deal with a crisis, it's him.

XXVII
RHEA

Darkness. My mind was shrouded in a fog so thick that every thought felt like a struggle. I remember waking up, faint lights piercing through the haze, bringing with them a pounding headache. My eyelids fluttered open, but the world around me remained a blur. Gradually, my vision cleared, and the first thing I saw was a small TV screen, split into four black and white images. A CCTV feed.

Panic set in as the images became clearer to me. The one on the top right showed a bedroom with Mike and a woman. It wasn't our bedroom. My heart sank as I watched the scene unfold. The woman left the room, and Mike collapsed onto the bed. My mind raced as I took in her appearance, realizing with a cold dread that she matched the description of Destiny from Mike's book. The woman he wrote about with such vivid detail. It couldn't be a coincidence. She was even wearing the same trench coat he described.

Someone had planted cameras in this house to spy on Mike and this woman. Clearly, they wanted me to see this. But who would do this? And why? The camera feed was suddenly obscured as the view shifted to reveal a person sitting in front of the screen. The light from the monitor cast an eerie glow on their face. I braced myself for the revelation, and as expected, it was me. I was the one tied to the chair, forced to watch this nightmare play out.

My arms were secured to the armrests with rough ropes that dug into my skin. My feet were bound to the legs of the chair, leaving me immobilized. A gag was tight around my mouth, stifling any sound I might try to make. It still feels as though it's wrapped around my skin. I felt groggy, as if waking from heavy sedation. My vision narrowed, locking onto the image of Mike on the screen.

Desperation flooded me. I struggled against the restraints, but they held firm, biting into my skin. My eyes darted around the room, absorbing the unfamiliar surroundings. Panic set in as I tried to piece together what happened. The last clear memory I had was of the note I received in the black envelope, instructing me to come to a certain street if I wanted to know the truth about Mike. I remembered standing there, waiting, anxiety gnawing at me, and then... everything went dark. Then, I found myself here, bound, and helpless, with no idea how I got here.

The phone on the edge of the table caught my attention, its screen lighting up with an incoming call. 'Mike calling' flashed on the screen. Now that I think about it, for someone who did so much to get me here, to leave my phone within reach, seems like a mistake. Hopefully they'll make another one. On the CCTV footage, I saw Mike, pacing up and down the room, his phone pressed against his ear. I lunged forward, chair and all, trying to inch closer to the phone.

The chair scraped against the floor, moving painfully slowly. The phone teetered on the edge of the table, tantalizingly close. With one final push, it tipped over, crashing to the ground. The screen shattered, and the call was dropped. Frustration bubbled up inside me, and I jerked violently, tipping the chair over. My head hit the floor with a sickening thud, and everything went black again.

When I came to, the pain in my head was excruciating. Blood trickled down my forehead, pooling on the floor beside me. I opened my eyes to a sideways view of the screen, blurred and disoriented. All the rooms seemed empty. Mike was gone. I hoped that he had somehow sensed my distress and had gone to look for me.

Consciousness eluded me, and I drifted in and out of awareness. Each time I woke, the world felt more surreal, more nightmarish. The ropes dug deeper into my skin, the gag suffocated me, and the sound of my heartbeat echoed loudly in my ears. Time lost all meaning as I lay there, helpless, and alone.

My thoughts wandered to Mike and the other woman. Who is she? Why is this happening? My mind circled back to Destiny from Mike's book. The realization that his fiction is more reality than I ever imagined made my blood run cold. My accusations were right, there's no denying that now.

The room grew colder, the shadows lengthened as the hours passed. I shivered, both from the chill and the terror coursing through me. The reality of my situation sunk in – I was trapped with no way out.

As my vision faded to black once more, a single thought remained clear: I must survive this. I must uncover the truth and escape this nightmare. But all I could do was endure and hope that somehow, someway, I would find a way out.

When I regained consciousness again, my eyes locked onto the TV screen to see Mike and the woman back in the house. Their bodies moved together in a rhythm I once knew so well, but now it felt foreign and painful to watch. The sight felt like a dagger to my heart, twisting with each movement they made. I blinked, trying to focus, and that's when I noticed – one of my hands was free. I hadn't realized that before. The entire armrest of the chair had broken off, probably from the fall I had taken earlier. Even though the knot was intact, I could move my arm. Hope flared in my chest, but it was a weak, flickering flame. I struggled to untie the knots, my fingers fumbling with the ropes. My body felt heavy, sluggish from the fall and whatever they used to knock me out. Every moment was an effort.

Finally, I managed to untie both hands and rip the gag from my mouth. I screamed for help, my voice raw and desperate, but there was no response. The room was a black void, save for the glow of the TV screen, then showing Mike and the woman. They were oblivious to my plight, wrapped in each other.

I forced myself to stand, though my legs trembled under my weight. I screamed again, but the sound was swallowed by the silence. The room had no windows, no visible door. Panic clawed at my throat. I stumbled forward, feeling along the walls, searching for any sign of an exit. The walls were cold and unyielding, a prison trapping me within.

My hands were slick with sweat, making it hard to grip anything. I banged against the walls, my fists aching from the effort. Inch by inch, I made my way around the room, praying for a miracle. Each step brought me closer to despair. My phone, lying on the floor, cracked, was completely dead, and still is. There was nothing – no door, no window, no escape.

I reached the last section of the wall, my heart pounding in my chest. I felt around, my fingers brushing over every surface, hoping for a hidden latch, a crack – anything. In my desperation, I banged my hand against the wall, and then it happened. Pain exploded through my hand as a nail pierced my skin, driving deep into my flesh.

I screamed, collapsing to the floor, clutching my wounded hand. Blood oozed from the wound, warm and sticky. Tears streamed down my cheeks, blurring my vision. I ripped off a piece of my t-shirt, gritting my teeth against the pain, and tied it around the wound in a makeshift bandage.

Leaning back against the wall, I tried to breathe through the agony. The pain was overwhelming, but I couldn't afford to pass out again. I closed my eyes, focusing on the sound of my breath, in and out, trying to steady myself.

The TV screen continued to play the scene between Mike and the woman. The sight of their intimate connection was a cruel reminder of my reality. Silent tears streamed down my face as I watched them, my heart breaking with each passing second.

I couldn't hear what they were saying, but the visual was enough to shatter me. Each kiss, each touch, felt like a betrayal, like a wound reopening every time it begins to heal. The way Mike was looking at her, the way his hands caressed her skin – it was all too much to bear.

I sat there, clutching my injured hand, watching the betrayal play out in front of me. The pain from my wound was nothing compared to the agony of seeing the man I love with another woman.

I'm not sure how long it's been since I've been sitting here. Mike has left and the woman is still in the house, but not visible in any of the camera feeds. As I lay against the wall, defeated, a thought occurs to me. The note. The black envelope that brought me here. It had promised the truth about Mike. And now, the truth has been delivered. But who brought me here? And why have they held me captive?

My vision blurs as tears spill down my cheeks. I don't have answers, only questions. The pain in my hand is a constant reminder of my predicament. I rest my head against the wall, trying to stay conscious, trying to keep the darkness at bay.

XXVIII
NATASHA

I watch from the doorway as Mike's car lights turn on and it pulls out of the driveway, disappearing into the night. The weight of our parting kiss lingers on my lips, but I can't dwell on that now. There's work to be done, secrets to uncover, and a plan to set in motion.

The house feels eerily quiet as I close the door and walk back inside. My eyes fall on the slightly titled Mona Lisa hanging on the wall. I adjust it, stepping back to ensure its level. But something nags at me. Grabbing the frame, I lift it off the wall, revealing a small hole. I turn the painting around. A key is hanging off the back, on a small hook. I take it, pushing it through the hole. The wall shifts – my secret door.

This house once belonged to my grandfather, a man shrouded in as much mystery as this place itself. He used this secret room to hide illegal ivory smuggled from Africa, trading it on the black market. Growing up, I never imagined this concealed space would be of any use to me. That changed the day I met Mike on the flight to London. From that moment, everything fell into place, and the room's sinister legacy found a new purpose in my own dark plans.

I push harder against the door, but something is blocking it from the other side. Panic surges through me as I force the door open, revealing a dimly lit basement. Rhea is slumped against the wall, barely conscious, a look of pure terror in her eyes. She must have blocked the door in her desperation.

I step inside, my eyes adjusting to the dark. The chair is toppled over, broken. Rhea, disoriented but alert, lunges at me with surprising strength. We tumble to the floor, her nails raking my face. I crash into the table with the monitor, sending it smashing to the ground. She tries to run, but I push her hard, sending her face first into the ground, in the corridor outside.

"Who are you and why are you doing this? What do you want? she screams, her voice raw with panic.

"Karma, bitch," I reply coldly, sending a kick into her ribs. She yells in pain.

I go for another kick, but she deflects it, causing me to lose balance and fall. She scrambles to her feet, eyes wild with desperation. Grabbing a lamp, she swings it at me. I dodge, but the lamp crashes into the wall, the bulb shattering into pieces. A shard of hot glass hits my face, burning my skin. I cry out, but the pain only fuels my rage. I charge at her again, grabbing her by the neck, chocking her with all my might.

My phone buzzes – Mike's ringtone. 'Flames' by Rehab. The distraction is enough for her to push me off and towards the doorway to the living room. I clip my shoulder on the frame and fall, but I'm back on my feet in seconds. The rage is boiling over. She makes a run for the door of the house. I chase after her, grabbing her by the hair, I drag her back towards the secret room. Her blood leaves a trail on the floor, a grotesque breadcrumb path.

Inside the room, I kick her a few more times, just for fun. Then, as I reach for the ropes, she surprises me again, locking me in a chokehold. We stumble around, crashing into walls, the room a blur of pain and fury. She tightens her grip, and my vision darkens. Desperation kicks in, and I manage to break free, sending us both flying into a wall.

Rhea fights back with a raw, primal strength. She claws at my arms, kicking and thrashing. I slam her against the wall, but she slips out of my grasp, diving for the door. I grab her ankle, yanking her back. She kicks me in the face, her heel connecting with my cheekbone. The pain explodes, but I don't let go. Instead, I pull her down, pinning her to the ground.

"Let me go!" she screams, her voice hoarse.

"Not a chance," I snarl, tightening my grip on her neck. She squirms beneath me, her movements frantic. I can feel her desperation, her terror. But I can't let her go. Not now, not ever.

She manages to get a hand free and slams it into my throat. I gag, the wind knocked out of me. She shoves me off, scrambling to her feet. I lunge at her, catching her around the waist. We crash into the wall again, the impact jarring. She elbows me in the ribs, and I gasp for breath. The struggle intensifies, each of us fighting with everything we have.

She grabs a shard of glass from the broken lamp, that's sitting by the frame of the door, and slashes at me. I dodge, but the glass slices through my arm. Blood wells up, but I ignore it, tackling her to the ground. She kicks me in the stomach, trying to break free. I pin her down, pressing my weight against her.

"Why are you doing this?" she sobs, her voice breaking. "What do you want?"

I slam her head against the floor, dazing her. The phone buzzes again, a cruel reminder of Mike's absence. 'Flames' by Rehab. The sound grates on my nerves, adding to the chaos.

Rhea seizes the moment, wriggling out from under me. She grabs the ropes from the fallen chair and swings them at me, the rough fibres scraping my skin. I grab her wrist, twisting it until she drops the ropes with a cry of pain. I yank her up, dragging her towards the wall.

Her eyes widen in horror as she realizes what's coming. She struggles, kicking and screaming, but I'm relentless. I slam her against the wall, pinning her in place. The nail pierces her skull with a sickening crack, and she goes limp. Blood trickles down, pooling on the floor.

"Oops," I whisper, stepping back. Her body hangs there, lifeless, like a grotesque version of the Mona Lisa. I tilt my head, mimicking her pose.

The room is silent except for my breathing. I look at Rhea's lifeless body, my mind a whirl of chaotic thoughts. "You know, when Mike and I first met... We had a very interesting conversation about Karma. Such a bullshit concept. What goes around, comes around. Only if life were that fair... If Karma existed, then, you and I... We wouldn't be in this situation."

I stare blankly at Rhea. "It's not fair you know... To kill someone's child. You shouldn't have done that. That child did nothing to deserve that..."

I pause, the weight of my words sinking in.

"And what was it for?"

Another pause.

"Nothing."

XXIX

MIKE

The night air is thick with tension as I drive through the streets of Bandra. My mind is racing faster than the car. Rhea's last known location, according to her phone, was Natasha's house. I grip the steering wheel tighter, knuckles white, trying to make sense of it all. What the hell is she doing there? Has she finally got her hands on one of those black envelopes and tracked down Natasha? Or did she follow me, putting the pieces together and realizing the affair? Each possibility is worse than the last, and my thoughts spiral into a whirlpool of confusion and dread. If she's seen me with Natasha, I'm doomed.

The streetlights blur into streaks of orange and white as I speed towards the bungalow. Memories of Rhea's strained face the last time I saw her flash before my eyes. I can't shake the feeling that something terrible is about to happen. The logical part of my brain tries to reason with me. Maybe there's a simple explanation. But the more I think about it, the more paranoid I become.

Why would Rhea be at Natasha's house? It doesn't make sense. Unless... Natasha. She lied about the whole DeVito

"

situation. I know for a fact that she never actually went and met him. I chose to keep quiet about it and try and make sense of it on my own before confronting her. And now I can't ignore the gnawing suspicion that she's hiding something else. What if this is all part of some twisted game she's playing? And to think that I was falling in love with this woman.

A cold sweat breaks out on my forehead. Natasha has always been mysterious, her past a murky blend of half-truths and evasions. The thought of her orchestrating something behind my back sends a shiver down my spine. I replay our conversations in my head, searching for clues I might have missed. Did she ever mention anything about Rhea? Did I overlook some hidden animosity?

I slam my hand against the steering wheel in frustration. Focus, Mike. I need to get to the bottom of this. The sound of the city fades into the background as I approach the familiar turn towards Natasha's house. The bungalow looms in the distance, a dark silhouette against the night sky. My heart pounds harder with each passing second.

As I pull up to the driveway, I kill the engine and sit in silence for a moment. The house is eerily quiet, the calm before the storm. I take a deep breath, trying to steady my nerves. My mind replays every possible scenario, each more terrifying than the last. I glance at my phone, considering calling Rhea one more time, but the dread in my gut tells me it won't make a difference.

I step out of the car, the cool night air hitting me like a slap in the face. The gravel crunches under my feet as I approach the front door. I hesitate, hand hovering over the doorbell, wondering what fresh hell awaits me on the other side. My thoughts are a tangled mess, fear and anger intertwining as I prepare for whatever comes next.

Taking a deep breath, I press the doorbell. The chime echoes through the house, breaking the oppressive silence. I step back, heart pounding in my chest, waiting for the door to open and reveal the truth. My world is on the brink of unravelling, and I can only hope I have the strength to handle it.

XXX

NATASHA

The smile on my face as I held the pregnancy test was bittersweet. Eight years ago, I was a different person, brimming with innocent joy. I look at Rhea's lifeless body, propped up against the wall, and begin my tale. My voice is calm, almost gentle, as if I'm speaking to an old friend.

"You know, Rhea, the moment you find out you're pregnant... it's indescribable. Another life growing inside you. A feeling you can't explain, only experience. I remember sitting on the bed, staring at the positive test, feeling a surge of emotions."

I close my eyes recalling the memory. The happiness that once filled me now feels like a cruel joke.

"I was so excited to tell Karan. I knew he would be just as thrilled. We'd been together for almost a whole month, and it felt like we were ready to take the next step. I even dressed plainly, in jeans and a t-shirt. Can you imagine? Me, in jeans?"

I chuckle bitterly, knowing Rhea can't hear me. But it doesn't matter; the words need to be spoken.

"I took an Uber to his place, nervous and excited. I wanted to surprise him, to share the joy. When I got to his door, I remember hearing music from inside the bedroom. His workout playlist. I thought I'd catch him mid push-up and give him the surprise of his life."

I pause, my gaze drifting to the floor. The memory of what came next still stings, even after all these years.

"I used the key I had gotten made, letting myself in quietly. I crept towards the bedroom, heart racing with anticipation. And then I saw it. Karan, mid push-up... on top of someone else. The woman he was fucking... was you."

I look at Rhea's face, searching for any sign of understanding, but there's nothing. Just the cold, empty stare of death.

"My heart shattered into a thousand pieces. I stood there, frozen, watching as the man I loved betrayed me with another woman. You didn't even look at me. You ran to the bathroom, like a coward."

I shake my head, the anger rising again.

"Karan tried to stop me, pleaded with me to stay. But how could I? My whole world had just crumbled. I ran out of that apartment, my heart breaking with every step. I threw up as soon as I hit the street. It could've been the shock, or the morning sickness. I'll never know."

I pause, remembering the sickness, the anxiety, the overwhelming grief.

"You knew he was in a relationship, but that didn't stop you. For one night of passion, you disrupted my entire life. You turned me into a murderer."

My voice breaks, the pain of that moment still raw.

"I went to the hospital, clutching the pregnancy test like it was my lifeline. The thought of raising a child alone, knowing that one day I'd have to answer the question,

"Where's dad?" It broke me. I couldn't do that to my child. So, I made the decision."

I remember lying on the examination table, tears streaming down my face as the doctor performed the abortion.

"It was always you, Rhea. You were the murderer, not me. The only way I could find closure was to make you understand what it feels like to watch the man you love with someone else. To have your family ripped away from you."

I lean closer to her, whispering in her ear.

"I'm glad you saw at least some of that, before this happened. I never intended to kill you. I only wanted you to suffer. Like I suffered. But maybe karma actually does exist, and it had other plans for you."

The doorbell rings, breaking the eerie silence. Not once, not twice, but repeatedly. I already know who's at the door. I stand up, ready to face the next chapter of my life.

"Now it's time for me to go get my 'happily ever after,'" I whisper to Rhea's lifeless body.

With a final look at the woman who destroyed my life, I leave the room, closing the door behind me. The past is done. Now, it's time for the future.

XXXI

MIKE

I'm standing at the door, ringing the bell repeatedly, my mind racing with possibilities. Why is Rhea's last known location here? I hope Natasha isn't hiding something. She lied about the whole DeVito situation. She could be lying about this. The lock clicks from the inside, and the door opens a few inches. I push it open a bit more and catch a glimpse of the mess inside – broken lamps, toppled tables. I squeeze through the half-open door and cautiously make my way inside.

Halfway in, I see Natasha sitting on the floor, her back against the wall, feet stretched out. The same feet that were blocking the door from opening. She looks to be in immense pain, and I rush to her.

"Natasha, what the fuck happened here? And where is Rhea?" My voice is sharp, my patience thin.

"She... she... left..." Natasha manages, her voice strained. She's barely able to get the words out.

"Why was she here? Where did she go?"

"She found out about us... She was... angry... I apologized... repeatedly but... she... wouldn't listen... I'm sorry, Mike…"

I take a moment to assess what Natasha is saying. Something doesn't add up. "I hope you're not lying to me, Natasha."

"Why would… would I lie… to you, Mike?" Her eyes widen slightly, but she quickly recovers, still struggling to speak.

"You lied about the whole DeVito situation. You said he was the one behind the envelopes and you took care of it but I know you never actually went to see him. I followed you that night. Why did you lie about it?"

Natasha looks flustered but quickly regains her composure. "I'm sorry, Mike. I only said that because… because I wanted to… put you at ease so you… so you could think clearly and sort out your issues with Rhea. I was only trying to help."

I'm not buying it. She's hiding something. Her response annoys me, but I decide to push the conversation under the rug to deal with the situation at hand. I inspect the wound on Natasha's face. "I'm having trouble believing that Rhea did this to you… She's not a violent person at all…"

Natasha remains silent. The wheels in my brain are turning, piecing things together. "Her last location shows this address, but that was hours ago… What was she doing here all this while?"

"Probably waiting… waiting for you to leave." Her answer is plausible, but my gut tells me otherwise.

"We need to get you to the hospital," I say, trying to shift focus. My priority is to find Rhea. To make sure that she's okay. I know Natasha is hiding something from me, she knows more than she claims.

"No, no… It's not so bad… Just please take me… to the… couch…"

I help Natasha to her feet, and we start making our way to the living room. I stop at the doorway of the living room, noticing a trail of blood. Too much for it to be from Natasha's wounds. It's leading to the end of the corridor.

"You lost a lot of blood," I say, more to myself.

"I'll be fine," Natasha replies.

I know this isn't Natasha's blood. I spot something else – the Mona Lisa painting is on the floor, resting against the wall. I take Natasha to the couch and help her lie down.

"Do you have a first aid kit in the house or bandages or something?" I ask.

"In the bathroom cabinet."

"I'll be right back, just stay here, rest." As I'm about to get up, Natasha grabs my hand.

"Thank you," she whispers, smiling slightly.

I walk out of the living room, stopping in the corridor between the living room and the kitchen. The blood trail leads to the wall. Sherlock Holmes can't leave a clue unchecked. I walk towards the Mona Lisa. I hear Natasha get off the couch and walk towards me. I sense her peeping into the corridor.

I rest my hand on the wall to bend down and take a closer look at the blood trail that ends there. The weight of my hand against the wall causes it to open, very slowly. I watch in shock as the wall moves to reveal a secret room. I see Rhea, sitting on the floor, right in front of me. I rush to her, trying to wake her up.

"Rhea! Rhea! Fuck! Rhea!" I check for a pulse. She's dead. I feel a surge of anger and disbelief. Turning, I see Natasha standing in the corridor, looking teary-eyed, and broken. I charge at her, grabbing her arms and swinging her against the wall.

"What the fuck did you do?" I demand.

"It was an accident," she pleads.

"My wife is lying dead in your house, inside a secret fucking room, with a broken chair on the floor, a smashed TV screen! Which part of this was an accident?"

"I never meant to kill her… I only wanted to punish her for killing my child."

All the pain that Natasha seemed to be in has disappeared. The words are flowing with ease. I take a moment to process the situation before accusing her of lying again. "Rhea killed your child? What the fuck are you talking about?"

Natasha bursts into tears and drops to the ground. I stand in the corridor, torn between the girl crying in front of me and my dead wife, not knowing what's true and what's not anymore. Rock and a hard place indeed. Kneeling down in front of Natasha, I try to make sense of her words.

"What do you mean Rhea killed your child? What are you saying, Natasha?" I want to say more, but the words won't come. Natasha tells me about Rhea and Karan and the entire incident that transpired between the three of them. My mind is reeling.

"Do you have any idea how fucked up all of this is? You seduced me to get back at my wife, you kidnapped her and made her watch us having sex, repeatedly… And then you killed her. All this because your boyfriend couldn't stay faithful?"

"FUCK YOU!" Natasha snaps back, and I'm taken aback.

"I'm sorry… I didn't mean to yell. I just don't like it when someone blames Karan. It's not his fault. He would never do that to me. He loved me. We were going to be a family. He would never betray me like that. Rhea seduced him."

I'm at a loss for words. This woman is completely insane.

"I had no other option, Mike. This was the only way I could make her experience the same pain I felt when she destroyed my relationship with Karan. I never expected to fall in love with you, but then I did, and everything changed."

I am baffled. "You manipulated everything. Every single thing. You knew exactly how to play me, to play Rhea. Everything from the moment you set foot on that flight was staged. And I fell for it, every step of the way. There is something horribly wrong with you... That video, the fucking thing that started this madness, the envelopes, the idea to send Rhea away... How the fuck could I be so stupid?"

"And that guy on the plane? The one who you blamed everything on? It was all one big lie, wasn't it? That's why you didn't want me to go after him. Fuck!" I stand up, pacing, trying to piece together the chaos that my life has become.

Natasha tries to speak, but I cut her off. "Don't even try to justify this, Natasha. You've destroyed everything. Everything!"

I collapse onto the floor, my head in my hands, overwhelmed by the weight of my situation. My wife is dead and my life is in shambles. The room is heavy with silence, broken only by the sound of Natasha's quiet sobs.

XXXII
NATASHA

Tears stream down my face as I sob uncontrollably. Mike sits on the floor across from me, stunned into silence, his face a mix of shock and disbelief.

"I love you, Mike. I'll treat you better than Rhea ever did," I plead, my voice breaking. "She's a lying cheater. You and I are meant to be together. We can be a family."

Mike's expression hardens, his eyes filled with confusion and anger. He gets up, pulling his phone out of his pocket. He starts dialling a number, turning away from me, unable to process the situation.

"Who are you calling, Mike?" I ask, desperation creeping into my voice. He doesn't respond. "MIKE!" I shout, my voice rising in panic. Still, he ignores me. "MIKE! I'M PREGNANT!"

That stops him in his tracks. The phone slips from his hand, and I can hear a voice on the other end repeatedly saying hello before the line goes dead. Time feels like it's standing still as he stares at me, eyes wide.

"I swear! I found out two days ago... I was waiting for the right time to tell you..."

"THIS! This is the right time?" he explodes. "You killed my fucking wife and now you're telling me you're pregnant. You're a fucking psycho, Natahsa!"

"We still have a chance, Mike. Our happily ever after? Let's run away, right now... The three of us can start fresh somewhere," I beg, my voice trembling.

Mike's disbelief turns to fury. He slams his fist into the wall with such force that I hear bones crack. Blood drips from his knuckles, but he doesn't seem to notice or care.

"Think about Karan, Mike. He needs his father," I say, desperation making me grasp at anything to keep him with me.

"Karan?" Mike's face contorts in confusion. "You need help. You're fucking crazy! He yells.

He picks the phone off the ground and starts dialling again. I know he's calling the cops. Panic takes over. I spring to my feet and leap onto his back, locking my arms around his neck. This scene feels eerily familiar, just like when Rhea attacked me before she...

I snatch the phone and hurl it to the ground. Mike tries to shake me off, backing up against the wall with enough force to make me lose my grip and fall. But I'm not giving up. I lunge at him again, but he shoves me back, sending me crashing into the wall again. The impact knocks the wind out of me, and I collapse to the floor.

Mike picks up his phone and storms out of the house, frantically making a call. I crawl towards the door, my voice hoarse as I cry out to him.

"Mike... Come back! Please... Don't leave... Mike... Don't make me kill another child."

XXXIII

MIKE

Sitting in the car across the street from Natasha's house, I can't help but feel the weight of the world pressing down on me. The street is quiet, save for the occasional hum of a distant car. Beside me, Ashish, my agent, is a reassuring presence. I glance at him, his face lit by the soft glow of the dashboard lights.

"Everything is set, Mike," Ashish says, his voice calm and confident. "Just remember your part."

I nod, my thoughts swirling. When we discovered that Natasha had lied about handling the DeVito situation, Ashish took control. They say money can't buy you happiness, but it can definitely buy you information. Ashish was able to get everything we needed from The Hulk to know exactly what Natasha was planning. It's commendable how a man as large as him could stand outside the window, recording a video without me spotting him. I was kept in the dark about certain parts of the plan to ensure a genuine performance. Acting has never been my strong suit. The plan was to kill Rhea and make it look like Natasha was responsible. The video was enough motive for it to seem plausible. Fortunately for us, Natasha was one step ahead, allowing us to keep our hands clean. With Rhea dead, I stand to inherit a significant amount of money with the insurance payout – enough to pay off the publishers their advance and take my time finishing the book. All the pressure would be gone. Ironically, I have just found the perfect ending for it.

Across the street, Natasha's house looms in darkness, a stark reminder of the chaos and deception that has brought us here. Ashish has been brilliant, turning every twist and turn to our advantage. Now, I just need to play my part – the heartbroken husband who went looking for his missing wife, only to find her dead in Natahsa's house. Although, now that she's actually gone, I wish there was another way.

"Ready?" Ashish asks, his eyes locking onto mine.

"Yeah," I reply, my voice steady. "Let's do this."

We remain in the car, reviewing the final steps of our plan. Ashish leans back in his seat, the hint of a smile playing on his lips. "You know, it's almost poetic how everything fell into place," he says, his voice filled with a mixture of satisfaction and anticipation.

"Do you think the cops will buy it?" I ask, needing the reassurance.

"They will," Ashish replies confidently. "The police will find Rhea's body, with enough evidence to prove Natasha was the one who killed her. Self-defence will be her only plausible explanation but with the secret room and the hidden cameras, no one is going to buy it."

I take a deep breath, the reality of the situation sinking in. "And when they start questioning me?"

Ashish chuckles softly. "You'll play the grieving husband to perfection. Think of it as your audition to play yourself in the movie. You were worried about your missing wife so you went looking for her, and tragically discovered her body. Your shock and heartbreak will be genuine because, in a way, it is."

I glance at Ashish, his calm demeanour a stark contrast from the turmoil I feel inside. "You really thought of everything, didn't you?"

He smiles, a glint of pride in his eyes. "That's what I do. You write stories, Mike. I make them reality."

We sit in silence for a moment, the gravity of what we've done hanging in the air. The sirens are faint but growing louder, signalling the impending arrival of the police. It's almost time to step into my role for the final act.

Ashish reaches into his pocket and pulls out a small flask, offering it to me. "A little courage," he says with a wry smile.

I take a swig, the burn of the alcohol grounding me in the moment. "Thanks," I mutter, handing it back.

As the sirens draw nearer, Ashish glances at me, his expression serious. "Remember, you found the body, you called the cops, and you're devastated. Stick to the script, and we'll both walk away from this clean."

"Yes Mr. Director."

I take a breath, bracing myself for the performance ahead. The plan is solid, and with Ashish by my side, I feel a sense of confidence.

Just as I'm about to step out of the car, Ashish stops me with a hand on my shoulder. "One more thing," he says, his voice laced with sarcasm. "Next time someone calls me a Danny DeVito look-alike, remind them that I'm at least five inches taller."

I can't help but laugh, the tension breaking for a moment. "Technically four," I reply, the absurdity of the situation not lost on me.

With that, I step out of the car, ready to play my part in the final act of this twisted tale. As the sirens wail and the lights flash, I take a deep breath, knowing that the story is far from over. But for now, the script is clear, and I have a role to play.

XXXIV

MIKE

Three months later, life has taken on a surreal quality. Standing at a small podium in a cozy London bookshop, I glance around, waiting for the reading to commence. The room is filled with eager faces, and there's a quiet buzz of anticipation in the air. As I sit there, I can't help but think back to all the events that led to this moment.

Ashish had warned me about Natasha from the very beginning, right from the flight, insisting that she was a bad idea. But then, in a twist of irony, he encouraged the affair, believing she would come in handy at some point to help us get out of the financial mess I was in. I didn't see it then, but Ashish's pragmatism was just another layer of the complicated web we were weaving.

When Natasha didn't show up at Ashish's house that night, after getting the address from the airline, we set the wheels in motion. We began to investigate the situation, piecing together the bizarre puzzle that was unfolding. It was through his digging that we found out from the Hulk – the burly, intimidating enforcer who worked for Natasha – that they had paid off my security guard to place the envelopes on my doorstep.

The Hulk also revealed that he had set up all the cameras in Natasha's house. They had watched our every move, capturing moments meant to destroy me. But the most shocking revelation was that he had kidnapped Rhea and brought her to Natasha's house. That's when Ashish realized the opportunity at hand.

If it hadn't been for Natasha and her twisted plan, Ashish and I would have had to consider a far darker alternative – ending Rhea's life to save my own. Natasha's scheme, as horrific as it was, ended up being the very thing that saved us, to a point.

That night at Natasha's house, when the cops and ambulances arrived, the story played out exactly as we had planned. Natasha was taken into custody, just as we expected. The unexpected twist was that Rhea, who we thought was dead, was actually not. She ended in a coma. For six long weeks, she lingered between life and death. It's funny how some things work out so perfectly in life. Rhea suffered a major concussion and severe brain damage, causing her to lose her memory. She remembered nothing from the moment she got into the Uber to go see her mother. I made sure that the story told to her was that she had a massive accident on the way to the airport and that was what landed her here. It worked. It was like someone had pressed the reset button on my life. All that was left of that horrific situation were the pages in my book, pages that were about to turn my life around, pages that would free me from all my financial troubles. Rhea's life insurance payout was no longer a thing of need. It felt like I had been given a second chance, a clean slate. Will Rhea ever get her memory back? That's a problem for another day.

I'm jolted from my thoughts as the reading begins. I glance at the eager faces before me. They listen intently as I read a passage from my book. The room is silent, hanging on every word. "Spirits" by The Strumbrellas plays softly in the background, adding a poignant touch to the moment. I've never felt this elated, this accomplished.

After the reading, I step outside the bookstore, a big smile plastered on my face. My phone rings – it's Ashish. I answer, happiness bubbling over as I talk animatedly. I step out into the street, still buzzing with the night's success. The world seems brighter, filled with promise.

My thoughts shift to Natahsa. Karma finally found its way to her. She ended up exactly where she belongs. I recall the hospital corridor. Long and sterile. I remember the one visit I made to her. To see what had become of the woman who helped me achieve this immense success. The door at the end of the corridor, a glass window revealing a glimpse inside. Natasha sat on a bed; knees clutched to her chest. She looked dishevelled, heavily sedated. She was never really pregnant, just a desperate attempt to hold on to a life that she had imagined. On the wall by her bed, a childlike drawing of three stick figures – a man, a woman, and a child – standing next to a house. Her past haunting her in every line of the crayon drawing.

Suddenly, I'm jerked back to reality. BANG! A car barrels though, sending me flying. As I lay on the street, my vision fading, my eyes move towards the bookstore's display window. There, in the centre of the window, is my book, given special attention for being a best seller. The cover depicts a silhouette of three people: a man in the middle, and two women on either side. The title is in a bold font, with blood dripping from the letters. It reads: 'KARMA IS A BITCH CALLED NATASHA' by Mikesh Kharbanda.

My life, my legacy, wrapped in the pages of a story too real to be fiction.

Everything slowly fades to black.

XXXV

EPILOGUE

I remember the moment I woke up in the hospital, the room sterile and quiet, save for the steady beeping of the machines. My eyes fluttered open, and there was Mike, sitting by my side. His face lit up when he saw I was awake, a mix of relief and something else – something I couldn't quite place at the time. The last thing I remembered was sitting in the Uber to go to the airport. After that, everything was blank.

"You're awake," he said softly, his voice trembling with emotion. "Thank God, Rhea. You've been in a coma for six weeks. There was a car accident, but everything's going to be fine now."

I tried to speak, but my throat felt like sandpaper. Mike squeezed my hand gently, reassuring me, his touch warm and familiar. "Don't try to talk yet. Just rest, okay?"

He told me about the book – how the publishers had loved it, how they'd given him a three-book deal. His excitement was palpable, infectious even. "I'm supposed to go to London in two weeks for the book launch," he said, his eyes shining with pride. "The doctor says you should be okay to travel by then, so I was thinking... maybe you could join me after the reading? We could spend some quality time together, talk about everything. I love you, Rhea. More than anything. I know we've had some troubles and I want to work through those. I want us to be us again."

I wanted to believe him. I wanted to believe that everything could go back to the way it was before. But there was a nagging feeling in the back of my mind, something I couldn't quite shake. Still, I nodded weakly, forcing a smile. "I'd like that," I whispered, my voice hoarse.

Over the next few days, I began to recover. The doctors we optimistic about my progress, and Mike was by my side every step of the way, attentive, and caring. But when I asked to read his new book, he hesitated. "You should wait until you're completely fine," he said, a note of caution in his voice. "It can be a bit intense, and I don't want you to stress yourself out, you've been through a lot. Just focus on getting better first, okay?"

I agreed, but the curiosity gnawed at me. There was something in the way he spoke about the book, something that made me uneasy. So, when Mike left for London, I did what I knew I had to do – I got my hands on a copy of his book.

As I read, everything came rushing back – the kidnaping, the affair, the fight, all of it. The memories hit me like a freight train, each one more painful than the last. The truth, raw and undeniable, was laid out before me in the pages of his book, and with it came a wave of emotions I could barely contain. Anger, betrayal, heartbreak – they all swirled inside me, threatening to consume me.

Two days later, I found myself sitting in my car, parked near the bookshop where Mike was doing his reading. I'd arrived a day early, intending to surprise him, but now, as I sat there gripping the steering wheel, all I could think about was Destiny's theory of Karma. How she never believed in Karma – not the way most people did. The idea that the universe would somehow balance out all the good and bad on its own seemed like a lazy excuse for inaction. If you wanted something, you had to make it happen, not sit around hoping the universe would drop it in your lap. The world didn't turn on its own; it needed a push, a nudge in the right direction. Good things came to those who didn't wait but who made their own luck. That was real Karma. And that, was what I was after.

I saw Mike step out of the bookstore, a big smile plastered on his face as he talked animatedly on his phone. He looked so happy, so confident, as if he had the world at his feet. My heart pounded in my chest, my hands trembling as I tightened my grip on the streeting wheel. I slammed my foot on the accelerator, the engine roaring to life as the car surged forward. The impact was brutal, sending Mike halfway across the street. The car came to a screeching halt a few feet away, the tires smoking on the asphalt.

I didn't move, didn't flinch. I just sat there, staring at the scene before me, breathing heavily. In the rearview mirror, I saw Mike's lifeless body sprawled on the ground, a dark pool of blood spreading beneath him.

Karma had finally caught up with him. And this time, it was on my terms. Mike was right about one thing – Karma is a bitch. But her name's not Natasha.

It's Rhea.